GUNMETAL GREYS

Also by T.J. Lockwood

THE 12 CITIES

Violent Skies
Urban Heroes

Origins

The Nature of Gods (2019)

GUNMETAL GREYS

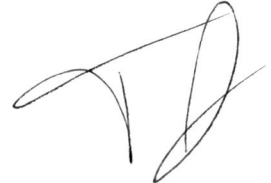

T.J. LOCKWOOD

**MECHA PANDA
PUBLISHING**

Copyright © 2018 by T.J. Lockwood

All rights reserved. This book or any portion thereof may not be reproduced or used in any manner whatsoever without the express written permission of the publisher except for the use of brief quotations in a book review or scholarly journal.

Cover Art by Nicole Roch and Tiffany John
Edited by Camille Gooderham Campbell

First Published in 2018

First Soft Cover Edition
ISBN 978-1-7751997-5-5

Mecha Panda Publishing
Coquitlam, British Columbia
www.mechapandapublishing.com

For bulk purchase inquiries or marketing opportunities, please contact marketing@mechapandapublishing.com

For all the secret family recipes which turned out to be frozen meatballs and barbecue sauce. Thank you for being both simple and delicious.

1
THE INFAMOUS BRIGAND

THE ROO IS FULL TONIGHT. To say that the smell of alcohol is pungent in the bar would be a grave understatement. If you sit back and close your eyes, you can hear the drunken rhapsody normally subverted by sobriety. My mama always told me that you could see into a man's heart when the liquor touched his lips. I don't know how accurate that is—the woman definitely had her eccentricities—but growing up, I found that she, more often than not, knew exactly what she was talking about. There just isn't a substitute for life experience.

"Well, aren't you just a cute looking thing. What are you supposed to be, sweetheart?" A man sits down next to me and spills a decent portion of his drink on the bar. Some of it splashes onto my vambrace. He reeks of whiskey, and not the expensive kind.

I'm too sober to be dealing with this.

"Don't you think you've had enough, Donny? You're wasting more than you're drinking." Charlie, the owner, takes the towel off her shoulder and sops up the discarded drops of drink. "Besides, you don't want to be messing with this one. Too much bite for you." She says those words like she is describing a snake rather than a person. "Keep your distance."

I can't help but chuckle. "Since when do you speak for me, Charlie?"

The tavern bustles around us with little concern about what's happening at the bar. Charlie shrugs and throws the towel onto the counter behind her. She smiles and turns to pour a drink. "I'm just trying to save this poor soul from a rather rude awakening. Unless the tiger is wanting to play tonight? Then I guess I can leave you two alone."

The man looks between the two of us and sloppily plays with his glass. "I'm right here, you know. It's rude not to answer a gentleman when he speaks to you."

It is my experience that those who claim to be gentlemen are usually anything but. "His name is Donny?"

Charlie nods in response.

I take a deep breath and turn my full attention to him for the first time. "Now, I think it's rude to call yourself a gentleman. A title like that should be earned with actions, don't you think—"

That's when I feel it: a full-on smack on the rear followed by leisurely footsteps. Someone just had the gall to touch my ass without permission. Donny looks on with great curiosity. He says something, but I don't hear him.

I don't finish what I'm saying; I don't even remember what it was I was going to say. Some lines just shouldn't be crossed. I spin around in my seat and see a tall skinny man in tattered jeans heading towards the washroom. It's loud in here but I can still hear him whistling to himself as he carries on without so much as looking back. Donny says something again. I still don't hear the words. Charlie probably says something too, but it doesn't matter. I'm charging in seconds.

One clean tackle from behind.

He falls face first into the jukebox.

Come to think of it, if Charlie had said something, it was probably along the lines of needing to calm down. The music cuts out as my target rolls over in time to take my fist to his nose. There's a scramble behind me. Someone grabs my arm. I follow the momentum as I'm pulled back and hit whoever it is that grabbed me. There's a loud thud as that person crumples to the ground. Then comes the uneasy silence. The bustle of the tavern is gone.

Charlie shakes her head and pours herself a drink as a couple of chairs slide back. "No matter how many times I tell you not to break the antiques..." The man who grabbed my ass pulls out a gun and pushes himself up against the wall. Charlie sighs. "Hey! No firearms in here. You know the rules."

His eyes are bloodshot and his nose is spewing red. "She started it. I'm just going to finish it."

I take a deep breath and meet his gaze. "Don't make me draw."

He shakes his head and raises his gun. "Draw? Draw what? I don't see any holsters."

I left my goggles at the bar, but it doesn't matter. I snap my fingers, raise my right hand and close my eyes just long enough for the flash of my vambrace to fill the room and then subside. The man is temporarily blinded along with the rest of the bar. I pull the metal trigger as soon as the weight of my gun fully materializes. One loud gunshot echoes, followed by a curse as the man drops his gun and holds his hand.

They say that it is impossible to see a Brigand draw. For the most part, that isn't incorrect.

"Damn it!" Blood seeps through his fingers. He feels it before he can see it.

I walk forward and kick his gun away to an empty corner. "I told you not to make me draw."

The gun in my hand is very real and I know that a lot of people looking on are confused at what they just witnessed. Normally I would have dealt with this the old-fashioned way. He moans as the patrons slowly funnel out the door. Donny is one of the first ones to stumble out. Only a few people end up staying.

"I don't think you understand what personal space is. Keep your hands to yourself or next time it'll be your—"

"Octavia?"

There isn't a single person in the bar that doesn't stop whatever they are doing right away. I know who's standing in the doorway. The scent of rain trickles in from outside. I step back and turn to face the robed man clutching a book in one hand and his glasses in another.

"Ezra."

He pauses for a moment and looks around the bar before walking in. His steps are heavy. The final few people that had stayed from before cautiously abandon their drinks and make a beeline for the exit. Ezra slides a stool out from the bar and takes a seat. "May I have a glass of water, please?"

Charlie reaches into a cabinet and pushes a button on the console. "You sure you don't want anything else?"

He shakes his head. "No, I'd need to pay for anything else. This will be fine."

The man on the ground starts to tremble. "A Chronicler? Are you kidding me? Then you're…"

I let go of my gun and watch as it disappears with another, less intense, flash of light from my vambrace. "I'm his Brigand."

Charlie shakes her head and starts wiping down the bar. "I swear, Ezra, brother or not, you two are bad for business."

Ezra smiles. "Just tally up the damages and estimate of lost wages. You will be reimbursed."

She shrugs. "You say that every time. The clientele changes each time I reopen. You two are just lucky there are enough people passing through here for me to survive. I know you're good for it, but money doesn't make the inconvenience go away, you know."

He sighs. "Then charge us more, Sis. Let us know what your inconvenience is worth."

The man growls under his breath. I can tell he wants to say something, but is thinking very hard on whether or not he should.

I turn away from him and retake my seat at the bar. "Leave before I change my mind and shoot something else."

"Bitch." He struggles to stand.

Ezra shakes his head. "Sounds like the man wants to lose another finger."

We all watch as he stumbles rather hastily out the door.

For a long moment, it's silent. Ezra takes the occasional drink from his glass; I pull out a rag and start cleaning my goggles. Charlie pours us a couple drinks—on the house, she says, but that just means the bill will be quite a bit heavier this time. She disappears into the back as Ezra opens his book.

"We should go." He turns the page. "Mason was

insistent that we not be late."

I take one final look at my goggles before replacing them on my head. "Fine by me."

He sighs. "And let's try not to shoot any more people on the way. You're supposed to protect me, not assault the citizens."

"He grabbed my ass."

"Just try, please?"

Ezra gets up from his stool and starts making his way towards the door. I put on my jacket, grab my hat off the bar, and follow. Charlie returns to her spot behind the bar as I step outside. The scent of rain is heavy, but there isn't a cloud in the sky. There is thunder, though. I can hear it booming below us. They say the flying cities are their own paradises, but I don't know about that. The day I call Hereford a paradise is the day the sun rises in the west.

Sometimes I think mankind should have stayed on the ground.

The skies can get mighty lonely.

2
THE DEPARTING CHRONICLER

My mama used to tell me stories about a city built to float on water. It was said to be a beacon of innovation and advancement for humankind. The end of that story is far from happy. All records in history tell us that this city eventually sank to the bottom of the ocean. In ancient times, this city was believed to have been blessed by the gods of Greek origin. Mama loved those deities; worshiped them almost. It was her opinion that we could learn the most about ourselves by looking back to that time in history.

Ezra believes in the Bible. The way he holds the cross around his neck says more than any words ever could. They say a Chronicler cannot have a religion—it would manipulate their judgment on how they perceive the events of history. I don't know about that. Ezra has always been impartial about what he sees. Still, no one at the Citadel knows that he prays. It is one of our many secrets. I, myself, don't believe in anything. Sometimes I think he wishes I did. That is just a hunch though. It's not something we have ever spoken about.

"Do you ever get the feeling that Hereford is dying?" Sometimes he says things like this.

I try to understand what he means, but most times I just have to smile and nod. "It's a flying city made of metal and constructed by people. It can't be dying because it's not alive."

He shakes his head. "Not the city; the people and their spirit. No one believes in our purpose anymore. You and I might be wasting our time."

"It's normal for societies to find new things to believe in, Ezra. I'd hardly call that dying." Occasionally, I paid attention in those history classes. "Just because people don't pray anymore doesn't mean they've forgotten about our traditions."

"It's just... I look around and see people taking so much for granted. We live in a place modeled after the most ideal time in human history."

I nod. "How does that old saying go? You don't know what you have until it's gone? That's the endless cycle. You can't make people go against their nature. Humanity will survive. We always have, and we always will."

He sighs. "I hope you're right."

We walk the dusty roads between villages for what seems like longer than it is. Hereford is not like the other eleven cities that loom above the Earth's surface. It's greener, and was built to replicate the world before all the advanced technology. They say the founders wanted to emulate a time of peace and calm in our history. I never really understood that. The surface below us is proof of the direction in which mankind is naturally headed. Creating a place based on the past will eventually catch up to the present. It's inevitable.

"Did we need to make any stops on the way back?" Ezra adjusts his glasses and brushes some dust off his sleeve.

I nod. "Just to see Grey and pick up my revolver."

He sighs. "I don't see why you carry that thing. It's primitive, and you have better technology at your disposal. I thought you were getting rid of it anyway."

"Just because it needed a tune-up doesn't mean I was going to throw it away. Technology can fail, Ezra, and I'd rather that not be the reason something happens to you." I adjust my hat. "It's dangerous down below. You remember what happened last time?"

He shrugs. "An isolated incident, I'm sure."

"Sometimes I think you're a little too optimistic for your own good."

He laughs. "That wasn't optimism, Octavia."

I pause. "Could have fooled me."

"Paranoia doesn't suit you. We always walk away from whatever scrapes we get into. I think I have more faith in you than you do."

"Don't mock my paranoia. It's what keeps you safe."

Just over the bend, the spires of the Citadel creep into view. This is the cathedral the other cities recognize—modeled after la Cathédrale Notre-Dame de Paris from the old world below. I don't like going there, but I follow Ezra and most of his business is done within its walls. The political interests there makes me feel extremely uncomfortable. I know I'm constantly being judged by people who think they are better than me.

Scholars and soldiers never seem to see eye to eye.

"You can wait in the market if you want." Ezra glances over his shoulder. "Go run your errand, and I'll meet you at the gates. I won't be long."

I shake my head. "You said Mason was expecting both of us."

"He is, but it's fine. He's not going to question it if

you're not there. Besides, you're fidgeting with that antique." He's talking about the Zippo in my pocket. "The clicking is atrocious. I don't know how you can stand it."

"We'll go together. It's fine."

He pauses. "I know you don't want to come. I wish you'd just say it."

But I should, so I will.

I take a deep breath as we arrive at the gates.

"Chronicler, it is an honour. Founder Mason is waiting in the council chambers. Will your Brigand be joining you?" The man standing at the gate is young. This must be his first assignment. He speaks to Ezra as if I'm not there at all.

"I don't know. Why don't you ask her yourself?" Ezra briefly glances at me before walking in.

The man now looks extremely uncomfortable. "Umm... yes, of course. Ma'am, will you be—"

"Yeah." One word, no embellishments, and I follow Ezra inside.

The interior of the Citadel looks nothing like its exterior. The stone figures lining the walls portray multiple eras and cultures, spanning everything from biblical prophets to Chinese philosophers. Mason is waiting in the room between the statues of Krishna and Augustus Caesar. He always is. The man seems obsessed with ancient Rome.

"Ezra, you made it. It's always a pleasure." Mason doesn't look up from the book in his hand. He stands in the corner of the room next to a table with many more books strewn open on its surface.

Ezra adjusts his glasses. "It is, thank you."

Mason glances up and then returns to whatever it is

he's looking at. "And of course, Octavia, it wouldn't be a party without you."

His words are dripping with sarcasm.

I decide not to respond.

Ezra walks forward and sets the book he had been carrying down amongst the others. "This was right where you said it would be."

Mason nods. "Then that new informant is proving to be rather helpful to our cause." He pauses, and picks up the book. "We have been looking for a copy of the Quran for decades. We can finally expand on our knowledge from the East." He looks up at Ezra. "I trust it wasn't too difficult to obtain?"

He shakes his head. "We met some unexpected resistance, but it wasn't anything Octavia couldn't handle. She did most of the work."

"Excellent. I am always happy to know our technology is not wasted on an incompetent Brigand." Mason steps back from the table and takes the Quran to his desk. "We've got one more for you. It's not time-sensitive like this last one, but it is definitely of great interest to us particularly because of its ties to ancient China."

Ezra nods. "Just tell us the details and we will be on our way."

Mason turns and grabs an atlas off the shelf behind him. "There is a man in Seattle who claims to know the whereabouts of the Goujian sword. It was uncovered in an expedition years ago and has since been lost."

I shake my head. "Seattle? That's a long way from China, Mason. Sounds like a bit of a wild goose chase."

"I assure you, Octavia, I have no intention of wasting our time and resources. This is the same contact that lead us to the Quran."

Ezra smiles. "Don't look so annoyed, Mason. She's just doing her job."

He shrugs. "Annoyed? Hardly."

The banter between the two of them continues, and I stop listening pretty quick. Talking about scholarly things is Ezra's game, not mine. I walk to the window and peer out at the green fields that make up the majority of Hereford's surface. It's hard to believe that such a place like this ever had to defend itself. I remember the day when St. Joseph's fell and Voltza very narrowly escaped the same fate. Hereford is a place of knowledge and worship. By all intents and purposes, we should have fallen, but there are secrets locked away in the past. My vambraces are proof of that.

History holds power. That is why these missions are so important.

3
THE CIRCLE OF LIFE

THERE ARE MANY PEOPLE WHO COME TO HEREFORD to better understand how the world used to be. For them it is a pilgrimage of sorts. This place is full of outsiders; some come and some go, but there will always be a few who stay from time to time. Grey is one of those people. He came to understand machines and stayed because of the green and the horses.

"She's a beauty, Octavia. Anyone who sees her should feel the prick of envy." Grey has always been good with mechanisms. "The model 10 will forever be a classic. Such a weapon would make Shakespeare sing."

I pause and watch as he carefully inspects his work. "Shakespeare never lived to see a gun like this one."

He shrugs. "No, but think of the possibilities if he had."

"Ezra says there is evidence of some modern art emulating Shakespeare. Different medium though. Film rather than theatre." I run my finger along the leather of the holster. "There was a time when people really loved their guns."

He smiles. "They still do."

"Not at quite the same magnitude."

The faint sound of sobbing catches my attention. I turn away from Grey and open the door to his shop. The sun is setting, but there is still enough light to see a little girl staring out into the street. Ezra is kneeling next to her with one arm on her shoulder.

"It's okay. This is normal." His voice is calm as he turns her away from the street to face him. "Everything has both a beginning and an end. That is the cycle of life."

I look past them and see exactly what it is that has made the girl cry. In the middle of the street lies the remains of a robin, and a crow towers over it with ribbons of flesh hanging from its beak. Death is the end for one but not the other.

"It's just... it's..." The girl can't speak. She doesn't look older than five.

Ezra smiles and offers his hand. "Hey, why don't you take me to your parents? When I was little, nothing made me feel better than a big hug from one of them."

The girl quickly hugs Ezra. For a moment he looks beyond awkward. I watch as he picks her up and begins walking across the market. Our eyes meet for a brief second before I turn around and walk back to Grey.

"Everything alright?" He places the revolver into its holster and sets a box of ammunition on the table.

I smile and nod. "Yeah. Just fine."

"Good, good." He starts pushing some buttons into the register. "Now, as always, I'm giving you the loyalty discount and throwing in a couple of things."

I pause. "What things?"

He shrugs. "Well, the ammo for one. Not that you'll use it, but it'll make that fancy gun belt of yours look mighty cool."

"Grey, I only need the six shots."

"Yeah, well..." He pushes the box closer to me. "I'm feeling generous. Just say thank you."

I sigh. "Really, there's no need—"

"Just let me do this." He looks away. "I don't have much, Octavia, and you have done more for me and this place than you ever needed to."

"Grey..."

He takes a moment then pulls a second holster out from under the desk. "Now, I know this is super primitive in comparison to those fancy things on your wrists, but this is from Harriet." It's a knife. "Neither one of us would be—"

"Thank you." Those two words seem to shock him.

I settle the bill, say thank you one last time, and then exit. Ezra is just outside with a cigarette in his hand. Smoking doesn't suit him. I've told him this multiple times.

"I see you've taken care of that thing you were dealing with."

He nods. "I did. Children are scared of what they haven't seen before."

I smile. "That goes for some adults as well."

"Naturally." He drops his cigarette and smothers it beneath his boot. "You ready to go, or do we have any more errands?"

"No, I think we're done here."

The sound of that crow pecking in the street still lingers in the distance. I don't ask Ezra about the girl. The man likes having his space, and I am not one to pry anyway.

Technology is complicated. Harnessing sound waves is one of the biggest breakthroughs of this century. Early on, mankind focused on the study of light, but eventually discovered sound was the key to instantaneous movement. I am not a genius, but I understand the methods. Sound study allowed us to develop everything from vambraces to shifters. A specific pitch at the right decibel has the power to manipulate molecules at the most basic level. It is also quite dangerous, and only to be used by those with the proper training. Playing with matter can get messy real fast.

Here we go again.

It's hard for me to stomach the feeling of travelling by molecular shifter. For a brief moment it feels as if my insides are rolling themselves inside out. Ezra stands quietly and watches. I look down at my hands and see them begin to fade. I disappear first and reappear safely in the cargo hold of a ship.

Ezra appears beside me in seconds. "See? We made it in one piece."

I shake my head. "This time."

I dislike being unable to control the tech that's rearranging my molecules.

"Chronicler, on behalf of Voltza and of the Maverick, we welcome you aboard and are equally honoured to assist in your mission." A short man in an armoured flight suit climbs down a ladder and offers his hand. "Captain Lincoln Dawes. It's an honour to meet one of the men who preserves our history."

"Let's not forget about the women as well." Ezra pauses, then shakes his hand. "A pleasure. As always, thank you for the assist. We know how busy the pilots of Voltza are."

Voltza, the mighty prison. Its pilots are feared by all who walk on the questionable side of the law. I met the Maverick once, even assisted when the prison was breached. The Earth shook, and everyone both above and below felt it. That was the day St. Joseph's fell and the twelve cities became eleven.

"The agreement between Voltza and Hereford still stands. We never forget our allies." Half of his body looks like it is made of metal.

Ezra pauses and then looks over to me. "We're getting dropped off just north of Seattle."

I nod. "Fine by me."

This is how every mission starts. I don't particularly pay attention. The pilots change but the missions stay the same. I take a seat on the floor and lean back against a crate. Ezra talks. He's a good—but awkward—talker. Dawes seems enthralled. I sigh, tip my hat down, and close my eyes.

I won't be getting much sleep on the surface.

4
THE LOCK WITHOUT A KEY

The cool air of the cargo bay becomes dry heat within seconds as the shifter powers up and sets me down on the planet's surface. I take a deep breath and lower my goggles. There's a lot more dust and wind than I was expecting.

Ezra materializes behind me and covers his face as a gust of wind hits him hard. "Holy..."

I pull the scarf from around my neck and toss it into his hands. "Yeah. It's a little nastier than the last time we were here."

He pushes his glasses higher on the bridge of his nose and wraps the scarf around his face. "This is ridiculous."

I look up and realize just where we are standing. "No, it's the exhaust from Voltza."

In the sky, far above us, the prison looms overhead. Looks like it is traveling west. I grab Ezra's arm and guide him south away from the dirty air. After a brief hundred-metre sprint we are out of its way.

"That was vile." Ezra unwraps the scarf and lets it hang loosely around his neck. "Disgusting."

I shake my head. "It could have been worse."

We both pause for a moment to get our bearings. Up ahead is a twisted concrete ramp which snakes the road around in different directions. We've come by here before, but I still forget which way to go.

"There used to be a lot of those down here. Apparently, it made getting around easier to manage with vehicles."

I nod. "Automobiles, you mean?"

"Yeah. They weren't such a bad idea until the fuel that powered them ran out." He starts walking forward. "Pretty dangerous, anyway. Highly combustible. The trucks on Hereford are much more efficient."

I smile. "I think I'd take my chances walking."

"No complaints here."

We make it about a kilometer down the road before I hear the echoes of gunshots in the distance. I stop and make sure Ezra is safely behind me. These roads are long open stretches. I don't like getting caught out here. If something goes down, there won't be much cover to shield him from the fallout.

"We should just keep going." Ezra grabs my shoulder and points towards an overpass. "At least until we get there."

I nod. "It's close. Can you sprint it?"

A look of slight horror appears on his face. "I'll try my best."

That's all I can ever ask for.

The gunshots don't let up. If anything, they get louder. I am starting to question whether or not going this way was a good idea. I like knowing what the guns are shooting at. Running into something blind has the potential for more than a little catastrophe.

A voice echoes in the distance. "Let me make myself absolutely clear. I have no intention of purposefully breaching these walls unless I have to. It is in your city's best interest to comply." A man dressed in military fatigues is shouting at the top of his lungs. The frustration in his voice carries alongside his words. "I'll only be an hour and then life can resume as normal."

More gunshots.

Ezra and I run up the concrete ramp until we make it to the top. I peek over the edge as he collapses beside me. "Jeez."

From here I can see the majority of the roadway ahead. Seattle's dome is up. Cities are only on high alert when threatened by something the local authorities can't handle. I take a few steps to the left and see what the commotion is. At the end of the roadway leading into the city stands a large group of people armed with what looks to be gunpowder rifles.

"This doesn't look good, Ezra." I turn. "They're blocking the way. How do you want to play this?"

He stares at me in disbelief. "You always ask me this question like I can provide some insight."

I smile. "Just trying to get your feedback."

"Just get them out of the way."

"You'll stay here?"

He nods. "I wouldn't dream of moving."

It takes me about thirty seconds to make my way down the ramp. It's always faster to follow gravity than fight it. As I approach, the little black dots seem to multiply. There are more people here than it looked like from our vantage point.

"Hey!" Almost everyone turns and raises their weapons. "Forgive me if I'm wrong, but you get more with honey than vinegar. Am I right?"

One of the men steps forward and clicks the safety off his handgun. "You need to back off. This is not your business."

I shake my head. "You guys are in the way of where I want to go. I think that makes this my business."

"What on Earth is going on back there?" As if someone uttered a magic word, the men draw apart, leaving a clear path to the man at the front. He adjusts his hat and takes a couple of steps forward. "Well, look what we have here." His accent is thick, Australian I think. "What the hell are you supposed to be?" He's got that look in his eye. I've seen it many times before.

I take a step forward. "Unimpressed."

"You wear it well, darling." He laughs and looks back to the city. "If you want in, then I'm sad to be the one to tell you that—"

"I think you should leave."

He looks as if I had just slapped him. "Excuse me?"

I stand my ground. "I'm not going to say it again."

"Do you know who you're talking to, girl?" The question comes from one of the men. "That's Jameson Polluck, and he makes his own way."

I smile and snap my fingers. "So, do I."

The burst of light is blinding. Gunshots sound

off. I stay low and make my way to Polluck. One kick and he falls to his knees. By the time the dust settles and everyone has regained their sight, I'm standing behind him with my gun pressed against the back of his head.

I've heard of Polluck.

He is as savage as they come.

I might be doing the world a favour if I put him down like an animal.

5
THE DETERMINED ROGUE

"Well, let's not get ahead of ourselves, darling. If you wanted me on my knees, all you had to do was—"

"No, there won't be any of that." I pull the trigger. The bullet grazes his ear and rips into the ground. Polluck clutches his head. My vambrace pulses and emits a low molecular field. As long as I hold onto the gun, it will remain materialized.

Not a single person has lowered their rifles. "Girl, we will put you down."

"Before or after I pull the trigger a few more times?" I snap my fingers with my left and watch as they cringe. Another burst of light flashes as a second pistol appears in my other hand. "I'd rather not have to make such a mess—"

Without warning, Polluck vaults himself back toward me. Those few seconds are enough to knock me off balance. By the time I regain my footing, he's standing across from me wiping the blood from his ear. "You *are* fun. Really got my heart racing. Not many people can do that to me. I want to know your name."

"We don't always get what we want."

He laughs. "There are no truer words."

Someone fires their rifle, and on cue all the others follow. I don't know how many times I pull the trigger as I jump for cover, but eight bodies hit the ground with loud distinct thuds. At least a dozen bullets hit me on the way. My armour-lined jacket has saved me more times than I can count. I take a deep breath and press my back up against a weathered concrete block.

I should have shot him.

"Hey, you guys wouldn't happen to know where I could find a washroom. Would you?" Ezra's voice carries just above a whisper.

For a moment the bullets stop, and that is when I move. "You idiot—"

Polluck turns and fires. My left cheek burns as I fall back to the ground. Ezra yells something. Might have been my name. I roll to my feet, vault behind a concrete divider, and ready myself.

"Octavia? That's an interesting name. How very... ancient." Polluck's footsteps crunch into the ground. "Was that so hard, darling? That's all I wanted to know." I carefully look out from cover and see Ezra standing about a hundred yards away with his hands in the air. Polluck smiles and steps over a couple of bodies. "Now, what are you supposed to be?"

The distinct sounds of metal hitting stone stops everyone in place. One of the men looks down at his feet then looks up and yells at the top of his lungs, "Grenade!"

The next few seconds is a rush of action. As Polluck and his men disperse, the grenade goes off. It's concussive and the resulting blast sends an uncontrollable ringing through my ears. I let go of my guns, feel their molecules dissipate, and vault out from cover straight towards Ezra. Polluck and his men are too busy clutching their heads to notice. Another loud thundering sound echoes behind me as I grab Ezra and drag him back towards the edge of the roadway.

"Octavia?" He pauses. "Thank God you're alright."

The ringing in my ears finally dies down. "Are you hit?"

He shakes his head. "No."

I take a deep breath and snap my fingers. There are frantic footsteps, loud yells and thundering crashes echoing just on the other side of our concrete cover. I take a deep breath before looking out. Polluck is nowhere in sight; neither are the rest of his men. Standing alone in the middle of bodies, playing with dirt, is a boy who doesn't look older than ten.

We make brief eye contact.

"Octavia, what is it?" Ezra sits himself up.

I'm not quite ready to stand down. "I'm not sure."

The dirt falls from the boy's hands as he walks towards us. "You're damaged."

I lower my weapons. "What?"

He points to his face. "You're damaged."

I let go of my guns. They disappear, and I pause for a long moment before lifting my goggles off my eyes. Ezra is standing now. He looks on as I step out into the open and walk towards the boy.

"Barely. Are you... damaged?"

The boy closes his eyes for a moment then shakes his head. "No, I don't think so."

It isn't until I am mere feet away that I see the grey in his eyes.

An android.

Ezra makes his way over, trying his best not to look at the bodies strewn around us. "What is your name, boy?"

The android looks up and blinks twice. "Maxim."

Ezra moves to approach the machine, but I hold him back. He doesn't argue. If there is one thing he has learned over the years, it is to trust me.

"And what are you doing out here?" My question goes unanswered.

The android turns towards the domed city and motions for us to follow. The sound of gears engaging fills the air as we approach the gate isolating the city. It opens remotely and I feel nothing but suspicion as the android steps inside and doesn't look back.

I turn to Ezra. "We need to be careful."

"Was that an—"

"Yeah, yeah it was."

There aren't many androids left in the world. The ones that remain can usually be found hiding in some hole where humans don't go. The fact that this one seems to walk as it pleases is more than a little concerning. Regardless, the way into the city is open. I start walking and Ezra follows. I can't help but tense up as the door closes behind us.

6
THE MAN WHO CALLS HIMSELF THE MINISTER

The streets are dark, and the air is noticeably thinner. Ezra's steps fall in line with my own. I don't know where this machine is leading us. The dome surrounding the city was made for protection, it but also blocks out what little sun can touch the ground. Ezra is nervous. He's fidgeting with something small in his pocket. The man has every right to be scared. I have no idea where we are supposed to be going.

I touch my cheek. The blood has dried. "Ezra, is this sword worth the trouble? I don't like where we are."

I feel trapped in this city.

He takes a deep breath and looks up from the ground. "The Goujian sword was discovered in a tomb back before the millennium. Records say that the blade was untarnished after being unsheathed for the first time in over two thousand years."

I nod. "Neat. That still doesn't answer my question."

"It's worth it." He pauses. "If we can find it."

The android stops and turns to face us. "My father is sleeping. We will have to go in through the back door." We're facing a very narrow-looking alleyway.

"The back door to what?" I walk right up to the machine. It doesn't look away.

The streets are dark, and the more we walk the darker it gets. The android pauses for a long moment and looks only at Ezra. "Do you know the Minister?"

The question lingers. Ezra quickly looks at me before responding. "No. Is that who we are going to see?"

The android nods. "You look just like him. He always wears black. Do you always wear black as well?"

Ezra hesitates to formulate an answer.

"Lots of people wear black." I move between Ezra and the android. "It's a pretty common shade."

It looks over at me and then shrugs. "But you don't."

"No, that's why I said—"

"Why don't you?"

The question lingers for a moment. I pause and then let out a sigh. "Just because it's common doesn't mean we all have to wear it."

The machine nods. "My father says there is no logic to humans. They are everchanging."

Ezra clears his throat. "He's correct. History shows many irregular patterns of violence and peace with momentary periods of—"

I hit Ezra in the arm and step towards the android. "Look, kid, we have places to be. I don't mind talking, but we need to walk and talk. A lot more gets accomplished that way."

"My name is Maxim." The android then turns and starts towards the alleyway.

Ezra shakes his head. "Octavia—"

"No." I start rolling up my sleeves as I follow. "This isn't the time for a lecture, Ezra. We're being led around a city in lockdown by a machine that could very well kill us."

"I think you are overreacting."

The memory of what happened with Polluck and his men is still fresh in my mind. "I don't think I am."

The street lights come on as we round the corner and come to a small well-kept courtyard. A building with a few steps leading to its entrance sits directly in front of us. Ezra is fascinated. He's no longer fidgeting with whatever is in his pocket. I'm waiting for the historical fact to burst out of his mouth. He gets excited whenever he sees something related to ancient times. Sometimes I can't help but make fun of him for it.

"This is perfectly replicated architecture from the twenty-first century." He moves past the android. "The brick work is fantastic. See the uneven grooves? Hand-made for sure. It's stunning. Simply stunning."

When he gets like this, I can't help but think that I am babysitting a child. Maxim walks up the steps, brings out a key, and opens the door. Ezra doesn't move. We're here for a sword and yet a brick wall stalls our journey. I roll my eyes and nudge him towards the door.

Ezra walks in. I follow close behind.

The gentle strumming of a guitar echoes in the

distance. Maxim picks up a small rubber ball and starts bouncing it against the door. Small paintings line the walls. To the right, an unlit staircase, to the left, a bright hallway. The rubber ball bounces as Maxim takes a seat on the stairs.

I go to speak but stop. Ezra has already started walking down the hall. The android stays, and the sounds of the guitar get noticeably more aggressive with each strum. My gut is telling me that we're walking towards trouble. I lower my goggles and snap my fingers.

Ezra turns just in time to be blinded. "What are you doing? Put the gun away."

I shake my head. "Just keep walking. Something isn't right here."

The guitar stops.

I quickly catch up to Ezra and pull him behind me.

"I always loved the word brigand. In this day and age, it is one of the strangest things to call a bodyguard. You know that, right? Your existence is a peculiarity." The voice comes from the room ahead. I only see the man who spoke once Ezra and I walk into a giant open space. It looks like a combination of a laboratory and a library.

Something catches Ezra's attention. He steps out from behind me and walks straight to the bookshelf on the left. My eyes never move from the man in the black robe sitting at a small table with a mug in front of him and a guitar on his lap.

"You're the Minister?"

He nods. "Yes, and you are a brigand. My, it has been a long time since I have seen a team from

Hereford."

I approach the table as the Minister adjusts his glasses and starts strumming again. "Are you the one who has the sword?"

The music plays. "You impress me, Brigand. Jameson Polluck is a very intimidating man. I think someone would have held a feast in your honour if you *had* pulled the trigger. That man is dangerous." He then glances over at Ezra. "And then this fellow comes out of nowhere and tries a rather comical distraction. You just can't make these things up."

I shake my head. "The sword, where is it?"

He laughs. "So peculiar. You do not disappoint."

Everything about this place has me feeling uneasy. This man, whoever he is, has the stench of a mercenary all over him. Ezra is still wandering around like a child. Sometimes he can be very aware; every other time, however, he gets distracted like a dog on the street. Maybe he was a goldfish in his former life.

"Where in the world did you get this? You have all three of the great lost holy books on your shelf." Ezra picks up a small black book and carefully flips through the pages. "I haven't seen a complete and intact Bible in years."

The Minister sets down his guitar, slides his chair back, and makes his way over to Ezra. "I've always had that book. It belonged to my father and his father before him. The best relics of history are those which were bestowed upon descendants. There is something about an heirloom that demands respect from those entrusted with it."

"What language is this?" Ezra squints and brings the book closer to his face. "I don't think I've seen this before."

"It's Spanish."

The bitter scent of coffee fills the air. A small machine in the corner starts dripping the distinctly dark liquid into a pot. The Minister walks towards it. Ezra follows, but I can hear another heavy set of footsteps in the distance. I turn back to face the hall we came from and see the edge of a shadow cast from around the corner.

Ezra talks, the Minister pours him some coffee, and as I step forward the shadow quickly retreats. I am ready for anything. There is too much about this place that I do not understand. Seconds turn into minutes, but my gaze doesn't falter.

"You know, there's no need to use your vambraces here. This is the safest place in Seattle." The Minister takes a sip of coffee. "You are my guest."

"Octavia?" Ezra walks to my side and puts a mug in my hand. "You need to relax. I like this place."

I shake my head. "Just because you like it doesn't mean it's safe."

Something here is making me feel uneasy. This man is out of place, and this place doesn't match the scenery. Then there is that shadow. It was much too big to have belonged to the android.

Ezra gives me a look I have seen too many times before. He's a trusting man, and I do wish he were a little more serious about his own safety. I take a deep breath and let go of the gun in my hand.

It disappears, and I find myself wondering if I've just made a mistake.

7
THE SWORD OF GOUJIAN

The laws of Hereford are much more independent than those of the other cities. Anyone who breaks the rules is dealt with by the courts and the people rather than Voltza and its prison guards. Outside the city, some may think this is a step backwards, but I strongly disagree. A community willing to hold people accountable is much more powerful than any institution. If someone has wronged you, then you deal with it yourself. Bureaucracy gets in the way of progress. Still, there are those who are trying to phase in democracy. They think they are so forward thinking, but history has shown us how democracy destroyed some of the most powerful nations from the inside out.

The Minister studies Ezra like Mason studies his artifacts. As much as my gut is telling me to leave, I can't. I go where Ezra goes. I made an agreement when I took the oath. A Brigand's duty is to protect their Chronicler. If I fail, then there will always be someone else to take my place. No one is irreplaceable.

Ezra talks with his hands. It's like he's drawing a

map in the air which only he can see, just to keep his thoughts organized. "You see, most people will say that the last big war is what made the surface like this, but it was actually the cities. The waste from the exhaust pipes and haphazard dumping greatly eroded the minerals in the planet's surface. The war just made some cracks, but passive forces helped change the landscape. That and the depletion of fuel resources..."

"And here we are." The Minister nods and takes another sip of his coffee. "The world is a strange place."

I stand with my back to a book case watching two men dressed in black talk about the world as if it were an object rather than the place we live. I'll be the first to admit that, of all the things Ezra rambles on about, I do find this interesting, but there is a time and place for these kinds of discussions.

Maxim enters the room and leans on the same book case where I'm leaning, only a few feet away. Every now and then he shuffles towards me and then stops like he is trying not to be noticed. I am cautious around androids, mostly because I don't know how they might react to certain things. Most humans are easy to read, but machines lack the typical tells and emotional responses that come with being flesh and blood.

"Do you need something?" I look down and see that he is only inches from my leg.

He looks up at me and then to the Minister. "No."

I step to the side.

He follows a minute later.

"You sure you don't need anything?"

He shakes his head. "I am functioning at full capacity."

"I see."

The Minister takes another sip of coffee and then sets the mug down on the table. "The sword you're looking for was here, but I gave it to another Chronicler. He offered me something I needed in exchange."

Ezra sits up straight. "Another Chronicler? That's impossible. Mason doesn't duplicate missions."

He shrugs. "The man was dressed just like you, and his Brigand was dressed just like her."

He's lying.

I push off the bookcase. "I thought you said you hadn't seen a team like ours in a long time. That is what you said, right?"

The Minister pauses. "Did I? You must be mistaken. Perhaps you misheard?"

I look to Ezra, but his eyes tell me that he doesn't remember. "I didn't. Besides that, we've been here for a couple of hours and now you choose to tell us this? Why would you waste our time like that?"

Ezra glances at me and then turns back to the Minister. "I would have to agree with Octavia."

The Minister laughs. "You would call having a lovely chat about history a waste of time? That surprises me, Chronicler. I saw the joy in your eyes. This wasn't a waste of time. Not to you, and certainly not to me."

Ezra's posture changes. It's slight, but those who know him will recognize that this is the first sign of him closing the doors to the outside. He slides his chair back and turns towards the door.

"Ezra?" I close the distance between us.

He turns to face the Minister. "It was a pleasure to meet you."

Maxim watches as Ezra leaves. The android looks to the Minister, who takes another sip of his coffee, and nods. I follow Ezra as I have done for years. This is one of those moments where I know it's best not to say anything. We walk and stop only once we reach the empty streets of Seattle. Ezra is unsure of which way to go. The air is thin, and while I think I know the way back, I'm not one hundred percent sure it's right. Behind us, Maxim has followed with the rubber ball clenched between his fingers.

Perhaps we should keep walking forward. We'll hit the dome eventually.

Maxim waits silently before motioning to the right. "It's this way."

The android then leads us to the city limits and opens the door, so we can leave.

It smells like it's going to rain soon.

Ezra continues, but I stop and look back at the city we had just come from. The doors to the giant dome close, and Maxim disappears behind the metal.

"Octavia."

I turn to see Ezra looking up at the sky. "Yeah?"

"Let's go home."

Failure always hits Ezra harder than anyone else I know. We've only come back empty-handed a handful of times before. When he's like this, it's best not to talk to him. The man has to cool off on his own before anything else happens. That is why I am more than a little nervous that he insisted on seeing Mason alone.

"Is it always this rowdy?" The beer in front of me is warm. "It's like a giant party in here."

Charlie nods and sets her towel off to the side. "This is normal after renovations. I always have a grand re-opening special."

I smile. "So, tell me, you aren't really sour when Ezra and I mess up the place, are you?"

She shrugs. "Honestly, not at all."

Someone slips a coin into the jukebox and the music changes from guitars to banjos. I didn't think it was possible, but the volume at the Roo gets even louder. A man stands on the pool table, hollers to someone across the bar, and begins to peel off everything he is wearing, one piece at a time.

"Oh, wow." I take another drink. "That poor table."

His shirt flies across the room.

"Fuck, dude." Charlie vaults over the bar and is stomping towards him in seconds. His pants go down. I look away, but it doesn't seem to faze her. "No, get down from there."

The banjo continues to play as Charlie expertly gets the man off the table, berating him as if he were a small child. I can't make out the words, but I wish I could. The man looks like he just stole a cookie from the jar and got caught by his mother.

"This is why I like Charlie's place. There's never a dull moment." The stool to my left scrapes against the floor. "Octavia."

I can't help but smile as I recognize the voice. "Valentin." We watch as Charlie grabs the man by the ear and throws him out with only half of his clothes in his arms. "What are you doing here?"

He shrugs. "Same as you. It's a drinking night."

Another man hops on the pool table and starts unbuttoning his shirt.

"Don't even think about it." Charlie stands at the door, fire extinguisher in hand.

I turn to Valentin. "Where's Asher?"

"Talking to Mason. Ezra?"

"Same."

Charlie walks around and resumes her spot behind the bar.

I don't even have to ask for a refill.

"Don't you two start anything. My tolerance for bullshit is done." Charlie reaches under the bar and pours herself a drink. "I swear I've seen more dicks than a prostitute."

Valentin laughs, and I can't help but chuckle as well. I'd wager that there isn't a person on Hereford who hasn't visited the Roo and had the time of their life at least once. It is a place to gather and a place to remember. The food ain't half bad, either.

8
THE BATTLE OF FORT HILL

I CAN HEAR THE SOUNDS OF HORSES in the fields behind the Roo. I used to have one when I was growing up, but I found her a new home when Ezra and I started working together. The constant traveling isn't good for family of any kind. I never really cared much about being grounded back then, but times change. I am not disillusioned, I know I'm married to my work. Still, I wouldn't have it any other way.

"This is the life, isn't it? Waiting around for the historians to decide where to dig." Valentin leans back on the bench and looks up at the stars. Even during the day, you can see them in the sky. "I have to admit that it's beautiful, though. Being above the clouds has its advantages."

I take a seat next to him. "It's rough down below. Ezra and I just got back from Seattle. A man named Polluck was trying to force his way in."

"Never heard of him. Was he amusing, at least?"

I shrug and point to the bandage on my cheek. "Almost got me. Ezra distracted him by doing something stupid."

He laughs. "I feel like I've heard this story before."

I nod. "Sometimes I look at him and think he's the smartest person in the world, and then he goes and does something stupid."

"And then you think to yourself that he must be the dumbest smart person there is."

I can't help but chuckle. "Sounds about right."

He sighs. "His older brother isn't any different—Asher is the same way."

"Now I know you're just messing with me. Asher is a lot of things, but I would never call him smart."

The thought lingers. Valentin takes a deep breath and then slumps down until the back of his neck is propped up by the bench. "He's a shit disturber for sure, but every now and then he'll say something profound. He doesn't give a damn about history, but when it comes to machines, the man's knowledge is second to none."

"He's like a child who just wants to play with his toys."

Valentin laughs. "Ancient machine toys, that is."

"I've missed this." He takes my hand and holds it.

"Me too."

The two of us sit together for what feels like an obscene amount of time. After a while, it seems like there just isn't anything else to talk about. Small talk only gets you so far. I watch men and women enter and exit Charlie's on and off for the next hour. Valentin has been swinging his legs back and forth for the last few minutes. Waiting is not something either of us like doing. Hereford is a big city, and as much as I like Charlie, her tavern is a small patch in the middle of nowhere.

"Asher and I came from Calgary. It's not that bad there. A little too isolated for my tastes." Valentin sighs. "The rodeo is still going strong, though."

"What were you after?"

He shrugs. "Some code machine from the Second World War. Well, a piece of it, actually. Turned out to be just a wild goose chase. Someone got there before us."

I turn slightly. "Sounds like what happened with us. Ezra was looking for a Chinese sword. Another Chronicler got there ahead of us, or maybe they didn't. I don't know, the contact was sketchy."

A moment of silence drifts between us. I've known Valentin a long time, and if there is one thing we can agree on, it is to leave the politics to the Chroniclers. We are Brigands. Our job is simple. No use in complicating it with things which do not concern us.

"It's the second time Asher's been duped, though. He was mighty pissed and rightly so. I'm not a fan of wasting time." He adjusts his vambraces and then pokes me in the side.

I catch his wrist. "What are you doing?"

"Just trying to pass the time." He laughs, but I don't see what's funny.

"Now, wait just a minute—"

An explosion erupts from the east. It happens without any warning. The plume of smoke is large enough to be seen over the horizon. Valentin and I are running towards it in seconds. He is a bit faster than I am. I try my best to keep up, but little by little he's pulling away. People start to scramble as if a gunfight had just broken out. Men and women step out of their homes with a weapon of some sort in their hands. Valentin and I are still running when the second explosion goes off.

"The Citadel."

Close by, I hear the sounds of stomping horses. Up ahead is a small open stable with a little boy cowering next to a bale of hay. There are no lights on in the adjacent house. Valentin keeps running, but I veer off the path towards the boy.

"Hey, kid." I take a moment to catch my breath. "Are there any horses here?"

"They all just..." He just stares at me with a blank look on his face.

"I'm not going to hurt you."

He bursts into tears and runs out of the stable.

I walk in and see four stalls near the back. A horse stands in one of them, chewing. I'm surprised it isn't at least a little spooked. I grab a saddle off a hook near the door and make my way back. There's another explosion. The horse still doesn't react. It sees me walking towards it.

"What in god's name are you doing?" A man stands at the door with a rifle in his hands and the little boy holding onto his leg.

I turn. "My name is Octavia—"

He shakes his head. "I don't care who you are. I asked what you were doing."

"I need a horse."

He lowers his rifle and begins walking forward. "Well, this ain't a charity."

I reach into my pocket and pull out a wad of cash. "How much?"

He shakes his head. "You don't want that horse. It's deaf."

Another explosion echoes in the distance. If there's one thing that never changes, it is the value of money, no matter the time nor the place.

The explosions have stopped, but that hasn't changed the fact that my heart is still pounding as fast as when the first one went off. I grip the reins and ride as fast as the horse will go. Valentin looks over his shoulder as we come up behind him. He slows his run and reaches out for the saddle. I stop just long enough for him to climb up behind. This horse is strong.

Neither of us says anything until we clear the horizon and come up to the Citadel. A fire rages on the first floor with flames spreading upward. Valentin jumps off the horse and runs towards the line of people with fire extinguishers and buckets of water. I want to move, but I can't. All I can think about is Ezra. We're lax on Hereford. There's only supposed to be danger when we leave the city. Things like this aren't supposed to happen here.

I take a deep breath and then ride ahead. The Citadel is made of stone, but there is still enough wood in the frame to fuel the fire. The inside of it must feel like an oven.

These flames don't look like they have any intention of dying peacefully.

9
THE DISAPPEARANCE OF EZRA KANE

WHEN I WAS A KID LIVING out on the borders of Hereford, one of the vegetation habitats caught fire, and those flames ended up engulfing about a quarter of the city. We are ready for a lot of things, and even though we strive to salvage moments in human history, we are still not adept at dealing with all the disasters that may come our way. I am not afraid of much, but fire terrifies me. By having replicated so many trees, we provided the perfect fuel source for the flames to spread. You'd think we would have learned how to deal with fire from that incident.

Valentin shouts to some people on the other side of the Citadel. The pile of empty fire extinguishers is slowly becoming a mountain. I jump down and tap the horse on the backside. It runs off into the distance and I return my attention to the chaos.

A small explosion erupts from one of the top floors. Valentin motions for everyone to get back as gravity pulls the debris to the ground. Someone yells from inside the Citadel. I am still frozen in place.

"Octavia!" Valentin calls my name. "I need your help."

I can feel this weight in my chest getting heavier with each passing second. "I can't."

He can't hear me.

Those two words were for myself, not for him.

I watch as he lowers his goggles and runs to the side of the building. He crashes his fist and his palm together and takes a modest step back as the flash of light engulfs the area around him. I look away, but when I turn back I see the full-sized shotgun in his hands. He takes aim and fires shell after shell into the wall. His reload is effortless; he drops his weapon, allowing it to dematerialize, and repeats the motion for another before it has the chance to hit the ground.

More people have gathered now, and that mountain of spent fire extinguishers is still expanding. Still, the crack of the flames signals that the fire is far from losing this battle. Valentin keeps shooting shell after shell, and all I can think about is Ezra. Standing here doesn't help him, but I can't will myself to move.

Sirens blare in the distance. One of the other districts must be sending help. I start to shake. The embers crackle and I'm quickly reminded of the events of my childhood; of the day I watched parts of me burn.

"Octavia, come on. I need your help." Someone grabs my arm.

Valentin.

I didn't see him run back. He pulls me, drags me, closer to the Citadel, but I stop him.

"I can't."

He shakes his head. "We don't have time for

this. Asher and Ezra are—"

"I know." I take a deep breath and start counting to ten in my head. "I know."

He sees me shaking.

I can't look at him.

He's judging me. There's no way he isn't. "Octavia, look at me." I don't. Then, in that moment, he takes my hand, and I do look at him. "It's going to be okay."

Another explosion erupts. This time it looks like one of the towers is starting to collapse. Valentin turns and pulls me away as the sections of stone start to fall. The sirens stop, and two large trucks pull up from the east. Those around can only look on as the tower crumbles completely. Neither Valentin nor I speak as the dust settles. There just isn't anything to say.

I've touched fire before, and felt it seep through the layers of my skin until the burning stopped, but the flames kept going. The scars have healed but the damage was already done. I can't feel the left side of my torso. Not even the best medical technology can repair nerve damage.

"Gone? What do you mean they're gone?" Charlie tosses a towel onto the counter behind her. "You're not making any sense."

Valentin takes a deep breath before starting again. "I'm saying that we can't find anyone. Mason, Asher, Ezra—the Citadel was empty."

She shakes her head. "So, you're saying that every

Chronicler on Hereford just up and disappeared during a fire?"

There is a long moment where not one of us says anything. Any patrons left in the Roo have already made their exit. Interacting with Charlie when she's angry is never a safe option. Valentin breaks eye contact.

I put my hand on the counter. "Charlie—"

She steps away from Valentin. "No, don't you dare finish that sentence. These are my brothers we're talking about. Don't tell me to calm down or that you guys are at a dead end. Your fucking jobs are to protect them!"

I take a deep breath. "Don't interrupt me. Especially when we're just as confused as you are. Like it or not, you do have to calm down, and we are at a dead end, but it doesn't mean we're done."

I've never seen Charlie look so small.

That isn't how I wanted to make her feel.

Valentin puts his hand on my shoulder and presses a button on his gauntlet. "Our first step is to make contact with the other teams. Mason had sent three of them out on missions before the Citadel fire."

I nod. "What about the others?"

He shrugs. "I don't know. The teams on Hereford aren't transmitting signals."

Charlie takes a deep breath. "What about the other Brigands?"

He pauses. "We don't know. They're not transmitting either. All I've got are three active signals on the surface."

"Before we do anything, we should meet with the

Maverick." I look down at my own gauntlet. "This might not be something we can handle ourselves."

"I know."

If there's anyone in the skies even close to being all-knowing, it is the Maverick. As the warden of Voltza, it is his business to know what is happening everywhere at all times. He isn't the nicest man, but he's resourceful, and for that reason alone, he is an essential ally.

I turn to Charlie. "We'll figure this out, okay?"

She doesn't say anything. I know she heard me, but I don't think she knows how to respond. Valentin and I both turn to leave. Our subsequent steps are slow and hollow. Hereford is supposed to be a safe place. Things like this shouldn't be happening here.

Ezra, where are you? Just be safe. Please.

10
THE MIGHTY PRISON

OF ALL THE TWELVE CITIES, not one of the others strikes fear into people's hearts like Voltza. It is one of the only cities which is constantly moving around the world. I have been there on several occasions and there is always relief each time I leave. First and foremost, it is a prison, and each inhabitant is trained to maintain order. The Maverick is not only the warden, but also the enforcer of the universal laws. His judgment is final, and his power is absolute.

Captain Lincoln Dawes walks towards us with a neutral expression on his face. He pauses, looks at the ruins of the Citadel and then back to Valentin and myself. His ship hovers steadily over our heads. "How many were injured?"

I clear my throat. "Five."

The pilot closes his eyes and slows his breathing. "That is five too many—"

"And at least seven missing." Valentin adjusts his gauntlets. "Our investigation into the events is pending, but we've lost contact with all the Chroniclers."

I nod. "And their Brigands."

Captain Dawes pauses for a long time before he opens

his eyes and waves his hand to the left. His ship starts a slow descent. "Has the council voted to give jurisdiction of this to Voltza?"

Valentin shakes his head. "They're still deliberating."

"That complicates things."

Behind us, a crowd has begun to form. Carriages, horses, and workers, all getting ready to rebuild. I recognize some of the faces. Valentin takes a deep breath and turns away from the pilot. He's frustrated and not very good at hiding it.

"As citizens of the Twelve, we have the right to invoke Order Thirty-Nine Delta. The Maverick is obligated to look into the potential kidnappings of four Chroniclers and their Brigands. They are all assets to the council of Hereford."

He nods. "There's a lot of red tape in that statement. It would be easier to let the council come to a verdict and invoke their own right to seek the Maverick's aid. If the order comes after, then the two files will create an administrative mess."

Valentin shakes his head. "People are missing, and you are concerned with paperwork?"

"Order is absolute." Captain Dawes turns as his ship touches down and opens its bay doors. "If you want Voltza's help, then don't invoke the citizen order."

Valentin goes to speak, but I pull him back. "Transport us there and we'll wait for the council's decision. That way we can get started right away."

"Voltza is no place for civilians."

I shake my head. "We helped defend the prison when it was about to fall. We're not civilians."

The Captain stops in his tracks. I can't see his face,

but the slight movement in his shoulders tells me that he's trying to stifle a laugh. I don't know this man very well, so I am not sure what to expect.

"Everything boils down to history, doesn't it?" Captain Dawes shakes his head. "Look now—"

"Captain." I take a deep breath. "Citizens of the Twelve Cities are missing, the Citadel is in pieces, and the council is reeling from its own losses. All we have at our disposal is history."

Valentin doesn't say anything as Dawes waves his hand in the air; his ship shuts down its engines completely. The cybernetics in his body are impressive. For a long moment there is only silence between the three of us. The crowd from before has dissipated and resumed scouring the Citadel for both survivors and clues to what happened. Hereford may reflect the past, but we are a connected people. Community outweighs any petty squabbles.

"You need to learn the meaning of law and order." Captain Dawes looks over at the rubble. "Neither of you comprehends the crimes Voltza sees. A lot of them are more severe than this. Our time is divided, and procedure keeps us focused."

Valentin shakes his head. "We have the right to seek an audience with the Maverick. You're just going to have to come to terms with the fact that we don't really care about your paperwork."

Captain Dawes sighs. "Are you invoking the order then?"

"I am."

He doesn't look at us. I know when someone is pissed off; Captain Dawes is furious. He waves his hand and motions towards his ship. The engines start almost instantly. "Well, let's get on with it, then. The Maverick is a busy man."

He walks up a boarding ramp, and we follow. The sounds of shovels and pick axes quickly become nothing but echoes in the distance. Then the doors close and there is only the hum of machinery. The Valerian takes flight and we are along for the ride.

I became a Brigand because there really wasn't anything else I was good at. I couldn't tend the fields properly after the fire killed fifty percent of my nerves. There is a lot about Hereford that shouldn't scare me, but it does. When Voltza was on fire, I didn't hesitate to pass by flames and take on the enemy. I can't explain what was different; it just was.

"Do you want to talk about it?" Valentin doesn't look at me when he speaks. His posture screams how awkward and uncomfortable he is.

I sigh and lean back against one of the crates in the ship's cargo hold. "It wouldn't help."

"Why not?"

"It just won't." I've tried talking about it before. Ezra tried to be sympathetic, but I ended up feeling more embarrassed than anything.

"Asher makes fun of me because I hate going into large bodies of water."

"What?"

"He makes fun of me because—"

I shake my head. "No, I got that part. I mean, why do you hate it?"

He takes a deep breath. "I've got some trauma in

my past that has taken me a long time to confront. Let's just say I'm not a fish, and I don't ever want to be one, either."

The ship takes a hard turn which knocks both Valentin and I sideways. I am quick to my feet, while Valentin struggles to stand.

Dawes' voice echoes through the comm speakers. "We're hitting unexpected interference. Voltza is accelerating back towards the continent. I am adjusting our course. We should be fine now."

He sounds less than enthusiastic.

"I bet he did that on purpose." Valentin looks over at the bay doors. "He seems like the spiteful type."

I take a deep breath and retake my seat. "He'll get over it eventually."

Several moments pass before we both feel the slight shift in gravity. The ship is descending. We must be getting close. Valentin adjusts his vambraces and looks at nothing but the cargo bay doors. "I haven't been to Voltza in a long time. Do you think it has changed?"

"I doubt it."

We touch down, and I hear Captain Dawes stomping from his pilot's chair to the cargo hold. He slides down a short ladder and waves his hand. The doors open as Valentin and I get ready to be greeted by whoever is on the other side. The sun is more than a little bright. We take our first steps as someone shouts in front of us.

"All weapons must be surrendered before disembarking." Five people in large armored suits stand before us with weapons aimed in our direction.

Captain Dawes walks towards us with a small metal case open in his hand. "Your vambraces."

Valentin shakes his head. "You can't be serious—"

"Valentin, it's fine. This isn't our city. We abide by their rules." I pause, then remove my vambraces.

Dawes places them inside. "These will be kept in the armory until your departure."

"That's fine." I turn to walk away, but am stopped by one of the guards.

"And the antiques on your belt." Captain Dawes motions to the holsters on my gun belt. "Knives and gunpowder pistols are still weapons."

I hand them over without question.

Valentin disarms as well.

"Thank you, citizens. Please, right this way."

The armoured guards start walking, and we follow. Their steps echo like hammers striking steel. Captain Dawes follows behind with the case securely in his hands. Voltza hasn't changed. Not even a little bit.

11
THE WARDEN'S WATCHTOWER

W**E ALL HAVE A ROLE WE WERE MEANT TO PLAY**, an identity we allow outsiders to see without compromising who we know we are. Brigands especially—we all have a front. Our presence and our mysteriousness allow us to help our Chroniclers. The less people know about us the better; however, none of that matters on Voltza. Records from all the Twelve Cities are stored in its mainframe. It is impossible to hide from the Maverick.

The deeper we go into Voltza, the more sombre it feels. This city is about as close to the opposite of Hereford as one can get. Everything is just a different shade of grey. The only colour stems from the blue of the pilots in their flight suits and the guards in their armour. The sun shines, but it feels cold. It's the wind. We're constantly in motion here.

Valentin doesn't stop looking over his shoulder. Our escort hasn't changed, but I can tell he's nervous. I am too, but I don't want to show it. It's a defence mechanism of sorts. I know it's futile, but it makes me feel better in the moment.

"I am needed elsewhere." Captain Dawes presses several buttons on his gauntlet. "You're about to enter the rehabilitation sector. Stay with the guards at all times."

We come up to a large building which looks about five times the size of the Citadel. Dawes veers off towards a tunnel station. Voltza's high speed trains are second only to RigMire.

The guards put on their helmets as we step inside.

The walls are orange and look like they are constantly shifting.

"Have either of you been here before?" One of the guards slows his pace until he is walking beside us.

I nod. "Yes, but only outside. During the fall of St. Joseph's."

He sounds very young. "You're in for a treat, then. Not many people get to see Voltza's arteries."

Valentin pauses. "Arteries?"

The guard nods. "Oh yes. This city is as close to being alive as technology will allow."

The lights pulse, and the walls shift from orange to yellow.

Without warning, one of the guards up front yells back. His voice is crackly and electronic. "Fynn, leave them alone. I need everyone's concentration until we enter section tango."

The guard next to us, Fynn, nods and tightens his grip on the rifle in his hands. "Yes, sir, of course." He pauses and then turns to Valentin and me. "Just keep your heads down and try not to make eye contact."

We come to a large set of doors at the end of the hall. Valentin and I look at each other as the guards stand in silence. There are no panels or speakers. We're waiting for something to happen— I'm just not sure what it's supposed to be. One of the guards in front raises a fist and opens his hand slowly. Gears shift as the door splits apart to reveal an open room with pods lining the sides. The lights pulse, and the walls turn green.

No one says anything as we walk forward. Each of the pods houses a person with cables connected to their joints. It looks like they should be hurting, but if they are, they're keeping it to themselves. We move, and their eyes follow. I can feel a pit forming in my stomach. A separate patrol of guards passes us along the lit path.

"Are they... okay?" Valentin looks intently at each pod as we pass by.

Fynn nods. "Oh, yes. They're fine. We're between modules. They will be asleep any moment now." He speaks in a whisper.

It's odd. Fynn is too chipper. His tone does not fit this place. One more pulse, one more colour change—purple—and those in the pods close their eyes. The lead guard raises an arm and everyone else lowers their weapons as we continue forward.

"This way, please."

Our guides herd us past another similar room and we come to a stop in front of a gated hall. Weapons and surveillance cameras line the walls. Valentin motions towards the ceiling. I look up and realize that the majority of what's above us is transparent. The ceilings are an illusion—nothing more than floors of pods and guard patrols. A loud buzz echoes as the gate opens. We step through a series of archways before coming out to a common area of sorts.

"Those were scanners." Valentin shakes his head. "I had no idea that Voltza had so many prisoners."

Fynn takes off his helmet. "Oh, those weren't prisoners. Those were rehabilitation candidates."

I pause. "What does that mean?"

A deep voice echoes from above. "It means that all those men and women are integrating themselves in our extensive social network program. It is proven to better help the troubled. We try to avoid locking people away if we can." A tall, thin, man walks down a large staircase. His suit is perfectly pressed and there isn't a hair on his head out of place. Several metal plates line the left side of his face. "Contrary to popular belief, Voltza is not solely a prison. Our rehabilitation facilities take up about half of the city's resources." Each step he takes echoes almost as loud as the guards in their armour. "Lieutenant, I will take our guests from here."

The lead guard salutes and then turns around. "Alright, you heard the Major. Let's get moving."

This place may be a prison, but its guards act more like soldiers than anything.

There is precision in their movements. Every step looks and feels coordinated. These are men moving like machines. The guards make their way down a hall until only Fynn and the Major remain. Neither Valentin nor I say anything.

"You need to stop meddling with the guards. You have your own duties to attend to." The Major's tone of voice has changed drastically. "This city isn't your personal playground."

Fynn shrugs. "I'd be careful with how you're speaking to me, Henry. I answer only to the Maverick."

"Technically, you answer to me as well. Don't be stupid now." The Major steps down and then redirects his attention to us. "My apologies for the wait. The Maverick is dealing with an important matter and has sent me to entertain you until he is available. Captain

Dawes tells me that you wish to evoke order Thirty-Nine Delta?"

I nod. "Yes, that's right."

"I will get the paperwork started, then."

"You kill all the fun, Henry. All of it." Fynn sighs and starts walking up the stairs. "Bureaucracy is going to be the death of us."

Valentin and I watch as he disappears up the stairway to the second floor. The Major sighs and tries his best to put on a face of confidence. He looks tired and overworked. No metal can hide that. "My apologies. Fynn is… an interesting one. He can sometimes come off as—"

"An entitled brat?" Valentin looks around. "That's what he seems like to me."

The Major nods. "I suppose that is the blunt way to put it. My hands are tied in these matters." He pauses. "But enough of that; please, allow me to give you a proper tour."

He walks, and we follow. I can tell Valentin is getting a little restless. Voltza feels like a different world in comparison to Hereford, but this is where we need to be. The Maverick is a powerful man, and we could use a powerful ally.

On Hereford, every step is heard in the crunch of gravel, but here it is the echo of metal. I miss the grass and the trees already.

12
THE COMPLICATIONS OF FAMILY

FOR AS LONG AS I HAVE KNOWN HIM, Asher Kane has always been a man of opportunity. I don't hate him, but I don't love him either. He and Ezra are very close, and as a Brigand I am able to watch both of them with relative distance. It is best we don't cross personal boundaries. I follow this rule as best I can. Valentin does the same. I think that's why we get along so well. The brothers go off and do their thing while we remain close by and do ours. Asher is a wildcard in a pack of fifty-two aces. He knows what he's doing and has a very unorthodox way of getting to his destination.

The Roo was empty, and Charlie was on vacation.

"Wait, don't touch it. We should examine the mechanism first." Ezra sat at a table across from Asher with a small machine between them hooked up to an old 1990s television set.

The air smelled of lavender, an experiment from one of the Chroniclers at the Citadel. Apparently, the plant had been considered soothing during the time before the twelve cities.

Asher shrugged. "What is there to examine? There are cartridges, cables, and buttons. We should push the buttons."

Ezra held his notebook. "I just want to make sure we hooked it up right. These connections are ancient, and what about these plastic rectangles with buttons?"

"There is only one way to find out—push all the buttons."

"Does Charlie even know we're here?" Valentin leaned against the bar with a glass of water in hand.

I shook my head. "What do you think?"

He smiled. "I think it might be time for me to switch to something stronger than water."

Ezra flipped through the pages. "No, let me just go over my notes one more time—"

Without a word from Asher, he pushed every visible button. The television lit up and music whispered through the speakers. This technology was old, but it still worked.

"Hey, looks like I was right. These are just a bunch of games."

Ezra paused as his brother started changing the cartridges and pressing all the buttons. "Wait—"

The machine froze. Asher hit the side three times and, with a flicker, the game resumed. "This is kind of cool. Nowhere near the level of holographic gameplay, though."

"You're going to break it." Ezra closed his notebook. "The buttons might be fragile."

Asher laughed. "What kind of idiot would make a fragile button? Buttons are meant to be pressed. If they lack durability, then they don't deserve to be called buttons."

I don't know if there was logic in that statement. It's hard to tell with Asher. Ezra leaned back in his chair and watched as his brother continued his tinkering.

"Want one too?" Valentin held up a bottle of vodka and reaches for a glass behind the bar.

I nodded. "Sure, why not?"

The Major walks slowly towards a large metal door. He rotates his shoulder and then moves inside. "This is our maintenance section. Everything is repaired here, from armour to appendages. It is important that we keep ourselves upgraded at all times."

We step inside and see a wall of mechanical limbs encased in glass. This looks more like a trophy room than a maintenance section. Valentin steps past me and starts examining the arms. He does everything but press his nose up to the glass. "Don't you find the decision hard, though? To cut off a part of you?"

The Major nods. "It's a sign of loyalty to our cause of administering justice and upholding the law. In the end, these are just tools. The upgrade is just as much a part of us as the body we are born with."

I pause. "I don't think I could do that. Not unless something was wrong with the limbs I have."

"Statistics show you are in the majority with that statement. People fear sacrifice. Only those with the will and understanding to do so are able to serve here. Voltza isn't a city, it is a duty—one we embrace and carry out for the good of humankind."

He believes in the words he has just spoken, and I think there is truth in them.

I go to speak, but stop as the Major looks away. He closes his eyes for a brief moment and then nods twice as if responding to someone.

"The Maverick is ready to see you." His tone of voice changes instantly. It's as if someone superior to him just walked into the room, but there are only the three of us.

He motions for us to follow and leads us back to the staircase from before. Valentin looks worried. He isn't good at hiding his discomfort. With each stair we climb, the smaller the rehabilitation centre looks below us.

"A word of warning: the Maverick has been dealing with a rather personal matter lately, so it is important to understand that whatever he decides regarding your claim is final. There will be no appeals. Is that understood?" The Major stops walking and turns—waiting to hear our answer.

Valentin pauses. "Wait a minute. How is that a fair—"

"We understand." I turn to Valentin. "Don't we?"

A moment of silence drifts between us. I am hoping Valentin understands what I do; this isn't the time nor the place to be arguing. We are both, quite literally, powerless here. The Major waves his hand, and a set of two heavy-looking doors opens before us. Ahead is another hall with a single room at the end.

The lights flicker, but the walls remain a very stark grey.

"Really? Can't you keep your hands to yourself for five minutes?" Charlie shook her head and stared at all the paintings on the back wall of her bar. "You're such a child."

Asher chuckled to himself as he stared at his

handiwork. Each painting was now slightly crooked. "Nope, just bored. Besides, your reaction was one hundred percent worth it."

"I am suddenly having second thoughts about feeding you."

That one statement was enough to make Asher go from confident to cautious. "You invited us to dinner. You promised food."

Charlie shrugged. "I promised food if you behaved."

Ezra nodded. "She did say that."

Asher paused. "How do you know?"

"Because I was there. Right next to you."

When all three of them got together it was interesting, to say the least. All of them were so different, and yet they still got along. I have always been used to waiting in the back corner observing. It's what I do best. The siblings would interact while Valentin and I would wait. Family is a strange thing. It's the answer to questions that make no sense whatsoever. It feels good when you have it, and like a void when you don't.

"Please, go on in." The Major motions towards the open door. "It's best not to keep him waiting."

I walk in first.

Valentin, second.

The Major does not follow. Instead, there is only the boom of the door closing behind us.

13
THE MAVERICK'S DETECTIVE

THE BATTLE OF VOLTZA TOOK A HEAVY TOLL on both the prison and on the volunteers from Hereford. We were able to fend off the attack quicker than the other two cities. It's as if the siege on the Citadel was an afterthought. St. Joseph's fell and Voltza was about to follow when the Maverick, for the first and only time ever recorded, asked the other cities for help. It was probably the most human he ever looked to the citizens. Five other brigands and I were the first to arrive. Our technology was primitive in comparison to what the soldiers of Voltza had, and yet it was clear that our arrival helped immensely. Explosions boomed as the city began to tilt, and I ran. I ran towards the nearest one and engaged the enemy. Valentin was there with me the entire time. Once our reinforcements arrived, the battle lasted no more than another hour.

Remember, Octavia, he's just a man with a few metal parts.

For some reason that thought wasn't as comforting as I thought it should have been.

The doors open to a room with more classic art in it than some of the galleries Ezra and I explored down below. These canvases were pristine and intact. Ezra would be geeking out if he saw them. One man sits behind a desk with a large screen active in front of him. It looks like he is watching footage of some kind.

"Henry tells me you have invoked the right to submit order Thirty-Nine Delta on the grounds of the incident on Hereford which occurred thirty-six hours ago." The Maverick does not look up from the screen in front of him. "Is that correct?"

The Maverick's real name is Elias Ridley. It's one fact everybody knows, but nobody talks about. There are some people who don't consider him a person. With over half of his body upgraded, and because of his infamously ruthless nature, his name is never spoken. His title is his identity, and his identity is the Maverick.

Valentin takes a moment before responding. "Yes."

The Maverick leans back in his seat. His eyes are cold. "And what makes you think you have this right?"

My mama always told me that speaking was an artform much harder to master than shooting bullets. Targets may move, and guns may jam, but people are complicated and unpredictable. The Maverick studies us. Looking into his synthetic retinas is intimidating. I don't know what I should expect from him. The room feels as if we are all sitting in the eye of the storm.

I take a deep breath. "Because we are citizens of the twelve cities."

He smiles. "Convenient citizens."

Valentin shakes his head. "What's that supposed to mean?"

"I think you know what it means, Brigand." The Maverick clears his throat. "You and everyone else from Hereford proclaimed you wanted the freedom to administer justice as you saw fit. I granted that and then some. I will not honour order Thirty-Nine Delta unless this changes."

The man sits there; his smile reverts to an expressionless visage. He looks both relaxed and tense at the same time.

I shake my head. "We don't speak for the council."

He nods. "And I don't expect you to. I am just telling you how the situation sits currently. Your city has a method of administering justice which does not align with the others. This makes matters complicated."

Valentin clenches his fists. "People are missing—"

"Don't mistake me for someone who doesn't care. I am a man of facts, and what I am trying to do is put everything on the table, so you can see the big picture as I do." The Maverick raises his hand. "You, sir, need to learn some discipline."

Discipline is harmony on any battlefield—soldiers understand this.

"Sir—"

The Maverick shakes his head. "You don't need to convince me of anything. This is how it is going to be." More keys click as the door opens behind us. "Captain Dawes has already submitted his reports and scanner data from his last visit to Hereford. I am not a man who brushes off his allies, but our aid must be limited. Do you understand?"

Neither Valentin nor I speak. Truth is, I don't completely understand, and based on Valentin's silence, I'm assuming neither does he.

Our silence doesn't seem to deter the Maverick. "My son will accompany you back to Hereford and help in your investigation, but that will be the extent of Voltza's involvement unless your city agrees to abide by the laws of the skies. Because of your city's status, we have no jurisdiction otherwise. Is that clear?"

Valentin goes to speak, but I cut him off. "Yes, of course."

Heavy footsteps echo as Fynn walks in, dressed in tactical clothing, with a long jacket draped over his shoulder. He nods to the Maverick and then rolls up a sleeve. I didn't realize it before, but both his arms are metal.

He runs his fingers through his hair and smiles not at the Maverick, but at us. "I'm rather excited. It's been a long time since I had a case to work on."

The Maverick nods and presses a button on his desk. "I trust you had time to review the details?"

Fynn nods, rubbing a small metal plate at his right temple. "Of course. I did that while we were touring the rehabilitation sector. This upgrade works very well."

"This is only an investigative assist. We do not have jurisdiction. No arrests and no active engagement. I expect a full report when you return."

Fynn bows slightly then looks at the two of us. "Understood."

The Maverick turns his attention back to the screen as Fynn motions for us to exit. It automatically closes behind us. There is a long moment of silence between the three of us. The echoes of machines are constant between levels. Voltza sounds more like a factory than a prison.

Fynn sighs. "Well, let's get on with it then. Dawes will take us back."

Valentin follows first. His steps are muffled by Fynn's. I suppose it's not a stretch to assume his legs are made of metal as well.

14
THE JESTER OF VOLTZA

CAPTAIN DAWES IS NOT IN A GOOD MOOD. For him to be anything other than neutral is rare. At least, I think it is. I haven't known him for very long. Men like this are easy to read. Their body language says more than words ever can. I have no doubt that his mood has something to do with the man sitting across from us in the cargo hold. I don't know who he is, but he seems to have a reputation. From the moment he came aboard, the atmosphere changed. Neither Dawes nor Fynn will acknowledge his existence.

I sigh. "We should contact the council when we land."

"And tell them what, exactly?" Valentin reaches under his jacket and pulls out a small metal container. "That we're on our own?"

I nod. "We need to keep them updated."

Valentin pauses and pops a mint into his mouth. "There isn't really anything to update them on. We're back at square one, only this time we have a walking tinman with us." He sighs and returns the small box into his pocket.

"I'm guessing no one ever taught you any manners

when you first started crawling. That's a shame. It really is." The man across from us looks up from the ground. "I bet you were an asshole in your previous life and it looks like you are in this one too. I don't know how that reincarnation stuff works. I'd look it up in a book, but I hate reading."

Valentin shakes his head. "Are you talking to me?"

He shrugs. "Well, I'm not talking to the lady, so by process of elimination, I must be talking to you. Why? Are you talking to me?"

I sit up straight. "Excuse me—"

The man raises a finger. "No need to defend the man. He should have offered you a mint, plain and simple."

Humans take joy in odd things. I can tell, by the smirk on his face, that this man enjoys confrontation. His cybernetics look crude in comparison to Fynn's and his jaw looks crooked, like someone has hit it a few times.

Valentin moves to get up, but I pull him back. "Don't. He's not worth the time."

"Now, that hurts—"

"Garrick, knock it off or I'll toss you out and you can freefall the rest of the way." Fynn slides down the ladder leading to the cockpit. "Don't test me."

He nods. "I wouldn't dream of it."

Fynn takes a deep breath. "Please let me apologize for him. He's not very good at knowing his place."

Garrick shrugs. "Oh, I know my place. I'm just a jerk. Why hide what you really are?"

I smile. "I suppose that's an interesting perspective to carry."

He nods, and then turns to Valentin. "And just so we're clear, we're not tinmen. We are human. We have flesh and we have feelings." He pauses and chuckles to himself. "Yeah, flesh with feelings."

Fynn clenches his fist, and Garrick immediately subsides.

I can see why Dawes wasn't keen on having him as a passenger.

The Valerian descends gradually then circles before landing. The moment we touch down, Dawes cuts the engine and then opens the cargo bay doors.

Garrick stands and approaches Fynn. "I'll find her."

He nods. "Or she'll find you. Be careful if it's the latter."

And just like that, Garrick steps off and walks out towards the broken highway of the number one. The doors close and Fynn looks to be lost in thought.

"Any more stops before Hereford?" Dawes' voice echoes through the speakers.

Fynn shakes his head. "No, let's get out of here."

"Wait, what the hell is this?" Asher paused as he stepped into the Roo for the first time after its third round of renovations. Ezra and I had already found our seats at the bar. To say the décor was different would have been a huge understatement. "These plates are laughable at best."

"It's high tea, and be careful with the china. That shit isn't cheap." Charlie motioned towards a free table. "Come on, we have lots to plan out."

Asher shook his head before making his way over. "You say that as if I'm supposed to know what it is."

Ezra sighed, left the bar and took his seat at the

table.

Valentin grabbed two shot glasses and a random bottle from the closest shelf. "Tequila?"

I smiled. "Aren't we supposed to have a lime with that?"

He sat down next to me and began to pour. "Nothing wrong with being a rebel."

"Is that what we are?"

"Always."

We each took a shot glass and drank until Charlie said it was time to go.

"What kind of place is this?" Fynn steps foot into the Roo and begins examining every inch of the bar.

Valentin goes straight to the pool table. "Anything and everything."

"Charlie!" I call out towards the kitchen, but nobody answers. It's not like her to leave this place unattended. "Valentin."

He nods and claps his hands together.

I move back towards Fynn.

"You don't have to worry about me if there's going to be a fight. I don't need a bodyguard."

Shouting echoes from outside the kitchen.

Both Valentin and I are running to the back door in seconds.

"What we need are answers. Clearly, we cannot be trusting the council. They've been in deliberation for too long." A man stands on a wooden crate surrounded by quite a few townspeople.

This feels like a gathering of some kind.

Charlie stands at the back with her arms crossed, looking less than impressed.

The man steps down and helps an older woman up. "We demand justice and that those responsible for desecrating our paradise be punished for their crimes. This is Hereford; the council obviously isn't with us, so we must handle this our own way."

I walk up to Charlie. "What's this?"

She pauses. "This is how things get out of hand."

"We are both judge and jury—"

"Hold up there, folks. I think we need to chill for a moment." Valentin walks past us towards the crate. "If the council is deliberating for this long, then this matter requires time."

The woman at the crate shakes her head. "Time? The longer we wait, the more time the terrorist has. People could die."

Fynn shouts from behind the crowd. "Action without evidence is not valid, no matter what set of laws you follow. This is how innocent people get punished for crimes they didn't commit."

Whispers begin to circulate amongst the crowd. No one is being subtle. It is obvious that Fynn is from Voltza, and it is also obvious that no one thinks he should have a say in what is happening.

I move past Charlie and stand next to the woman on the crate. "Those responsible will be brought to—"

"Brigands!" One of the Citadel guards, covered in dust, runs towards us from up the main road. "We found survivors!"

The whispers turn to chatter, but I don't process the words. Both Valentin and I are following the guard before anyone else has a chance move.

15
THE OLD MAN'S PROXY

I'VE DONE A LOT OF RUNNING IN MY LIFE. So much that it has become about more than just getting from point A to point B. I've learned to run with purpose. Without purpose, we are nothing. Mama always said bullets never lie; they go exactly where they're meant to go. There's nothing tricky about them at all. A straight line. As Valentin and I run, I wonder if I am going to like what I find. Hereford has seen bloodshed before, but I don't think we're ready to see it again.

Fynn runs past us in seconds. I don't know if it's his cybernetics or if he's just a fast runner, but he quickly leaves us trailing as he becomes a small figure in the distance. I've only ever seen riders on horseback travel so quickly. I'm just hoping he won't overstep when he gets there.

Several people are following behind us.

Charlie is one of them.

I know she wants to help, but she needs to stay back.

Valentin shouts to one of the guards, who motions to the inside of the Citadel. Fynn is standing tall, tapping a small screen on his left arm. I take a moment to catch my breath.

"We should keep civilians off the premises." Fynn's eyes shift from blue to red as he looks up and down the structure. "This place isn't safe. Structural integrity is severely compromised. If there are survivors, then they are deep underground."

Valentin shakes his head. "What do you mean by underground?"

"Octavia." Grey emerges from the ruins with a coil of rope slung over his shoulder and more than a little dirt on his face. I'm surprised he's left his shop. "Over here!"

I quickly make my way over. Behind him, both townspeople and guards are hammering small metal stakes into the ground. "Someone said there were survivors."

He nods and looks down at the giant crater next to us. "There are—at least, we're hoping there are. We're making a lot of assumptions. One of the guards went to find you and Valentin off before we could confirm anything. We can hear voices—"

"There's an entire intertwined system of tunnels below." Fynn is still examining his screen. "It runs through the length of the city."

Grey looks as if he has seen a ghost.

He doesn't stop looking at Fynn.

"Grey?"

He looks genuinely scared. "What is that *thing* doing here?"

I grab his shoulder. "Grey, are you serious? I didn't take you for—"

"I have to go."

I watch as he leaves without saying another word.

Valentin walks up to me. "What was that all about?"

"I have no idea."

Fynn steps past the people readying the ropes, and approaches the broken statue of Augustus Caesar. He looks up and then down towards the base. "And here I thought Lantis was a mysterious place."

Valentin and I walk over as he pushes the name plate on the statue's front. A loud click echoes as the statue slides backwards into the wall, revealing a narrow staircase.

"You've got to be kidding me." Valentin pulls a small light from his belt. "I didn't even know this was here."

I nod. "I don't think any of us did."

Fynn shows us his screen. "There are over ten levels. See these lines? Wall divisions."

"How can you see that from up here?" I quickly look up to him and then back to his arm.

"I have some of the most powerful upgrades on Voltza. My job is to survey a crime scene, assess the timeline of events, and assign targets for the pilots to capture."

Valentin pauses. "So, the Maverick sent us back with his investigator."

Fynn shakes his head. "No, he sent you back with his son."

Everything about his tone of voice screams that he is annoyed. Valentin goes to speak, but decides against it as Fynn starts to descend the staircase.

I have seen the remnants of many cultures over the years. Every time I've asked Ezra about the more obscure ones, his usual reply is that he doesn't know. So much of history has been lost, and it is impossible to say if we will ever be able to get it back. As Fynn, Valentin, and I walk through these dim halls with nothing more than the puny lights in our hands, it is clear to me that there is more history in this place than any of us realized.

The little screen on Fynn's arm flickers. "The walls are getting thicker; my scanner is having a hard time mapping this place out."

There is a very audible scuffle behind us.

Valentin claps his hands together and draws his weapon. Fynn stares into the flash of light and then carries on unfazed.

"Octavia! Valentin!" Charlie's voice echoes.

Valentin relaxes a little and calls back. "We're down here."

I shake my head. "What are you doing?"

He shrugs. "She's coming either way."

Charlie quickly sprints up to us and leans against the wall to catch her breath.

She's alone—no one else descended with her.

It's probably for the better.

We walk forward until we come out to an open area similar to the Citadel atrium above. Fynn puts a hand on his holstered weapon and advances to the left. The sounds of movement carry to us from the distance. Valentin goes right as I keep moving forward. Charlie stays close behind me.

"This place looks old." Charlie kneels and touches the floor. "Older than anything in the museums."

"Ezra would be geeking out if he saw this architecture." I take another step, but stop as my boot comes down on something. I move back and see that my light is centered on a small vinyl figure.

"What are those?" Charlie moves ahead and sees a pile of them scattered beneath a broken shelf. "They're like tiny people."

I pick up the figure and inspect its beady eyes and oversized head. "Sculptures maybe? There are so many of them."

Charlie picks up a small dog figure. "They look... kind of cute though."

We continue on into a narrowing hallway. Something stormed down this way, leaving nothing but broken display cases and scattered artifacts in its wake. I snap my fingers and summon a pistol. Music begins to play further down. Something doesn't feel right.

"What is that?" Charlie motions to walk ahead, but I stop her.

"I don't know, but you should stay back a little. It might be dangerous."

Without warning, the halls fill with light and I find myself adjusting to the change in brightness.

Fynn, calls out from behind us. "I found a generator. That should make it easier to see."

Up ahead, the music grows louder and louder. I advance quickly. The walls are an off-white and house many shelves and pictures. I don't recognize any of these things. I round the corner and come to another hall with several doors on either side.

"Hello?" I call out, but no one answers.

I take a deep breath and open the first door. It looks like nothing but a shrine to automobiles. The second is red and gold with a giant 'M' plastered on the wall. The music is coming from the third.

Valentin moves past Charlie until he is right next to me. "This place is like a labyrinth."

"It's creepy, is what it is." I put my hand on the door handle. "I quite literally have no idea what to expect."

The next few moments feel as if they are happening in slow motion. The door opens, and before I can react, there is a hand on my shoulder and a slight discomfort building in my left side. My reaction is simple; someone is on me.

I hit them back and take aim until I find myself staring into a familiar set of eyes. "Asher?"

He looks up from the ground, drops the knife he's holding, and puts his head in his hands, "Oh fuck. Oh fuck. Oh fuck. Octavia, I didn't mean to—"

"Asher, what are you—" I take one step and then feel the dull discomfort in my side. I look down and see the bloody slash. For a moment, I am more confused than anything. The blood is seeping out of me, but I can barely feel it.

I know I should be reacting differently, but I don't. Behind Asher are several Chroniclers slumped against the walls, unconscious and injured. That is when I see him face up and not moving.

"Ezra." His name is the only thing I can will myself to say.

Nothing else matters.

I just need to know that he is alive.

16
THE MEANING OF HONOUR

EMOTIONS ARE IMPOSSIBLE TO INTERPRET, so I don't even try. Valentin feels the same. It's why we've never minded being forgotten about when Asher and Ezra have things to take care of. We've always understood.

"Octavia!"

I feel Valentin's arms around me as I drop to my knees. It's strange. There is a combination of pain and numbness in my side. *I should be screaming, shouldn't I?*

I am too calm.

Why am I so calm?

Asher staggers back and hits the wall at full force. I didn't mean to hit him so hard. It was all a reflex.

"Frick." It's the weirdest feeling; knowing you're injured, but not being able to feel it fully. There's only pressure. "I'm fine."

Valentin shakes his head. "Don't move."

Fynn is next to me in moments, with his hand only inches from the wound. "Your nerves are unresponsive. This is worse than what your body is registering."

Everyone is talking to me, but my eyes are only on Ezra. "Is he alright?"

Fynn lifts the edge of my shirt, studies the gash, and then quickly covers the wound with his hand. His eyes shift from brown to purple.

"What are you doing?" Valentin tries to push him away, but he doesn't move.

"Patience." His eyes shift from purple to red.

Charlie moves past me to her brother. "He's fine."

I can feel a warmth building deep down beneath my skin, a brief moment of discomfort and then nothing. Fynn removes his metal-plated hand, crusted in red, and I watch as it sizzles in the air.

It looks hot.

My wound is patched.

Just another scar touched by fire.

"Get off of her!" Valentin reaches around me and pushes Fynn backwards. "What are you trying to—"

I take a deep breath. "Valentin, stop. I'm okay."

His eyes trace the scars on my body. I can feel his gaze as it travels. For a long moment, he looks sad. "Octavia..."

This scene, despite its uncertainty and mountain of unanswered questions, is familiar. Things aren't perfect, but we are together, and right now this feels like the only thing that matters. Charlie helps her brothers as both Valentin and Fynn help me to stand. Now all we need to do is find some answers.

My mama once told me that the biggest secrets in life were the ones out in the open for everyone but you to see. Things can be hidden for a really long time if no one is looking for them. The network beneath the Citadel is vast. Fynn wasn't exaggerating when he said it spanned the length of Hereford; it's like there's another city below the surface.

"The subject is delicate. I'd rather not discuss it at this time." Mason sits at a table in the Roo with several Chroniclers gathered around him. His robes are torn, and the scratches on his face tell the story of a physical skirmish. Those who were severely injured went with Charlie to the hospital.

Ezra hasn't woken up since we found him, and I would be lying if I said this wasn't affecting me at all.

"Delicate?" I shake my head. "We find the city's Chroniclers hidden in an underground hole and you still don't want to fill us in on what happened? We could hear those explosions across Hereford."

Everyone looks at me as if I've just said something sacrilegious.

"Octavia." Asher starts with my name, but has trouble getting the rest of his thought out. "It's… complicated."

I shake my head. "You were scared enough to attack the first thing that came through that door. It's not complicated."

Valentin steps forward. "Where are the other Brigands?"

I nod. "And the three teams on the surface?"

Asher looks to Mason, as if waiting for a cue of some kind. One doesn't happen; at least, not that I can see.

"It would make sense that they were the real targets." Fynn looks down at his screen. "Given the circumstances of who is accounted for, and the fact nothing was really taken from the Citadel, this feels like the objectives were unconventional."

Mason shakes his head. "What are you talking

about?"

Fynn sighs. "Why would someone want to blow a hole in the city of history and knowledge and then leave all of that history and knowledge intact? Three Chronicler-Brigand teams are unaccounted for. Otherwise, we are missing a lot of body guards."

Mason nods. "They are the least of our concerns."

"I don't understand how they could be the least. They seem rather significant to me." Fynn pauses. "The evidence points towards—"

"Why are you here again? I was not notified the council authorized Voltza's intervention." Mason slides back his chair. "Your presence here is insulting. We deal with our matters our own way. The Maverick would never allow this."

Valentin looks to Asher. "You and several other council members were in a hole in the ground, so Octavia and I acted. This was the best way we could think of to gain aid—"

Mason slams his fist on the table. "Typical. Your job is to protect, not to think—"

I lean forward. "Don't say another word."

His glare turns to me. "I'm sorry, I don't think I heard you right."

The air feels heavy.

"You're really pissing me off." My chair scrapes the ground as I stand and make my way towards the door. "No one was here. We made this call so we could open avenues to protect those we are supposed to. Your criticism isn't warranted."

"Your only job is to take a bullet when we need you to. You can't possibly comprehend what you've done." He pauses and points to Fynn. "This is the first step to losing our independence. If history has taught us anything, it is how outsiders ruin societies."

Mason's words are followed by a thick moment of silence.

I look at Fynn, who does nothing but observe the scene. He does not look offended; he merely studies.

He's following the Maverick's instructions to the letter. Doesn't matter. No one has the right to be treated this way.

"What are you talking about?" I shake my head. "Without our allies, we are nothing."

All eyes are on me.

Asher steps forward and then turns to Mason. "That was uncalled for."

The laws of Hereford are different than those of the other cities.

I lower my goggles and snap my fingers. "Mason, you and I have a problem now. How about we settle it the traditional way."

Mason flinches. "Octavia, that's enough!"

"Pick your weapon." I motion towards the door. "And we can settle this outside."

The tension is fragile. I can feel Mason's fear. He's the kind of man who enjoys talking without the promise of action. He is not better than we are; he will never be better than we are. His chair slides back as he scans the room. I don't know what's going through his head, but he looks panicked. He must know there's no winning this.

"No." He straightens his back and steps around the table. "You're going to stand down."

I raise my weapon. "You speak of our ways and then deny me my traditional right to challenge you? You're a coward—"

"Octavia." *Ezra*.

He and Charlie enter from the kitchen. His eyes are bloodshot, and he looks more than a little tired.

"Ezra."

He raises a hand. "Please, no more violence."

The fatigue in his voice is evident. Still, I won't let Mason talk to us this way. It's not about me—it's about everyone else he has slandered as well.

I look to Ezra and shake my head. "I'm sorry, but what he said was unacceptable."

Everything seems to slow down for the next few seconds. I sigh and take aim.

Mason is the only one who screams as I pull the trigger.

17
THE HOT-TEMPERED FUGITIVE

Hereford is the closest city to the stars. This place is my home, always has been and always will be. I grew up running through the fields of synthetic grass and climbing the genetically modified trees. I am a citizen, I am a Brigand, and I am slowly losing my love for this city.

People keep saying my name like they can control me, and it is starting to piss me off.

"Octavia." Valentin walks to my side and puts a hand on my shoulder. "I think he's had enough."

"You lunatic! Have you lost your mind?" Mason stumbles to his feet. "You could have killed me!"

I nod. "And I still could, so sit your ass down."

Some people believe they're entitled to respect. Mason is one such person. I am not one for regret. Any decisions I've made in my life have helped shape both who I am and my reputation. This is no different.

Fynn leans back in his chair and starts a slow clap. "I like this city. There's never a dull moment here."

Charlie steps forward. "This is hardly the time for humour."

He stops. "I wasn't meaning to be funny. I was just speaking my mind. I haven't been here longer than a day, and already there are so many secrets. I like the mystery."

Mason brushes himself off. "This is none of your concern."

Fynn smiles. "I'm not sure what you're referring to. Do you mean the attack on the Citadel? The sorry state of the city's Chroniclers? Or perhaps you're talking about the fact that Hereford doesn't seem to know whether or not it should look towards the future or stay entangled in the past?"

There isn't a Chronicler in the room who doesn't look at least a little bit offended. Mason shakes his head. "I want you to leave—"

I laugh. "And I want answers, but it seems like neither of us are going to get what we want. He stays."

Ezra looks towards me. "Octavia, please—"

"No. I feel like I'm missing something big, and it bothers me. I wasn't there to protect you this time, and that made me feel like I'd failed in the one job I've always been good at. What the hell is under the Citadel, and why were you all cowering there like you had seen a ghost?"

"Because there were ghosts." Asher hops over the bar and pours himself a beer. "We were lucky. The men who stormed the Citadel had twentieth century guns and came at us with primitive technology."

"And they won. Plain and simple." Ezra looks at Charlie. "They only took the Brigands. Our visiting friend might be right about a few things."

Asher gulps down half his beer. "The tunnels beneath the Citadel are a tomb of sorts. They hold the pieces of history we've found that do nothing to benefit mankind today. If anything, some of what's there would hurt progress. Humans have some dark moments in our past."

Valentin sighs. "You're telling us you hide these things away so no one knows our past? It doesn't seem right to pick and choose what to remember."

"You two have said enough." Mason walks towards Ezra. "This goes against the creed."

Charlie steps between the two of them. "You, sir, need to calm right down."

It isn't an exaggeration to say that Mason towers over Charlie. Fynn chuckles to himself. The other Chroniclers start to whisper in the background.

This isn't getting us anywhere.

Sometimes the best thing to do is just walk away. My mama always told me that people say horrible things when they're angry. Anger almost always leads to regret. I don't want to be one of those people who sit back and reflect on things which could have been, rather than looking forward to how things are.

There's a void between Ezra and I; maybe it was always there, but this is the first time I've noticed it. I wonder if Valentin feels the same about Asher. Of all the things we've talked about, our feelings about our Chroniclers have always been off limits. The night air is cool, and the roads are empty, but the Roo is still as lively as ever. The debate hasn't slowed down one bit.

Between Mason, and Ezra, I needed some fresh air. Walking the fields has always been good for my sanity. The flowers should be in bloom soon. Then the scent of lavender will carry subtly in the wind.

I just had to get out of there.

"Octavia?" Grey sits on one of the benches with a drink in his hand. He looks tired and a little bit out of place.

"Oh, Grey, what are you doing here?"

He smiles. "Drinking. It feels like one of those nights."

I nod and take a seat next to him. "Tell me about it."

He pauses and hands me a can from the box at his feet. "My wife is hysterical and I just... I don't know what to tell her. She doesn't feel safe. We left Lantis because of the crime. I like this place. I don't want to relocate again, but the explosions have me on edge."

I pull the metal tab and take a sip. "Fair enough."

He leans back and looks up at the stars. "Do you think we'll be alright?"

"Life goes on. Nothing we can do about it."

He shakes his head. "That's not what I mean."

A light breeze flows past us, and I find myself mesmerized by the stars above our heads. Hereford is one of the highest of the twelve. Most people will go their entire lives without seeing a sight like this one. I wonder if we will ever make it to the stars. The skies feel just as grounded as the world below.

I take another drink.

"What I mean is," he sets his own drink on the ground, "do you think we are allowed forgiveness when we die?"

My fingers start to tingle. "I don't—"

"Because I've done a lot of things I'm not proud of." Grey reaches under his jacket and pulls out a pistol. "And there's still more to come."

The can falls to the ground as my hands start to shake. I have no grip. He turns to me and I move off the edge of the bench. It's hard to focus. My steps are clumsy.

"Octavia." He stands and starts walking towards me. "I am forever indebted to you. I need you to know this. You have to know this."

There is a look in his eyes which I have never seen before: sadness. He reaches into his pocket and screws a silencer onto his weapon. Everything feels as if it's moving in circles. I can't activate my vambraces.

"Grey..." I don't know how, but I'm falling. The ground hits me hard.

I reach for the gun on my hip and pull it free from its holster. Grey stands over me and takes aim. I do the same, but my hands won't stop shaking.

"You should pull the trigger, Octavia." He glances towards the Roo. "Someone might hear the shot and come to your rescue."

My arm feels so heavy.

It takes all my strength to pull the trigger.

Click.

Nothing happens.

He kneels and takes the weapon from my hand. "Guns are loyal to their masters."

The ground comes out of nowhere again, but this time the darkness comes along with it. There are footsteps, there are words I can't make out, and then there is nothing.

18
THE SECLUDED BLACK BOX

THE AIR SMELLS LIKE CHERRY SODA. It's the only recognisable thing about this room. The ground is cold, my back is firmly pressed against a stone wall, and I can't see anything. My jacket is gone, along with the weapon Grey messed with. There are no lights, but my vambraces are still on my forearms.

Why didn't they take them?

I lower my goggles and snap my fingers. The brief burst of light gives me a glimpse of something horrific. If I saw what I think I did then I don't want to snap my fingers again. I take a deep breath and hold my pistol tightly. This is no ordinary room.

It looks like someone was torn apart in this room.

"Your sound signature is harder to pinpoint than the others." A voice booms through a speaker above my head. "Mind doing that again for me?"

I look up towards the sound. "You've got to be kidding me."

My heart starts to beat faster. I can feel myself getting increasingly anxious with each passing second.

"Is that a no, then?" The person sounds way too chipper for a situation like this.

"Who the hell do you think you are?"

In that moment, intense light floods the room and I drop one of my weapons to cover my eyes. Not even my goggles can compensate for the sudden shift in brightness. It takes a minute to adjust, but when I do, I see exactly what I'd had a glimpse of before. Small pools of viscous liquid and shredded clothes are scattered around the room. There were other people in here before me.

Where did they go?

"Octavia." There is a lone speaker overhead with various nicks and cracks around the casing. It looks like it's been shot a few times. "Your cooperation would be most helpful."

Grey.

I shake my head. "Being helpful to a kidnapper doesn't sound very attractive to me."

He sighs. "No, I suppose not, but it would save us from the unpleasantries."

The room feels like it's shifting beneath my feet. The movement is slight, but it's there. I step back as the speaker is lowered into the center of the room.

I take aim. "What is this?"

The speaker begins to rotate. "As a Brigand, I thought you knew your history."

Nothing I've encountered ever looked like this room. "It is the Chronicler's responsibility to know about history. All I need to do—"

"Is protect. Is that what you were going to say? Bodyguards are the best recorders of history because they're always watching—observing—what is happening in the world."

"I thought we were friends, Grey."

The speaker turns. "We will always be friends, Octavia."

I shake my head. "Friends don't kidnap each other and—"

"I know." The lights go off. "But I had no choice."

I shuffle backwards as far as I can until my back hits the wall. My boots are sticking to the ground. I try not to think about what I've just stepped in. A loud bang echoes on the other side of the room. It sounds like something heavy just hit the ground. I take a deep breath and try my best to steady my breathing.

Then there's a piercing howl and I don't hesitate to pull the trigger.

Some people will insist that Hereford is the most dangerous of the cities to visit, based solely on how we uphold our laws. In my mind, it is simple—you wrong me, I deal with it my own way. This is how we've always lived. I don't know how you can call that more dangerous than a city floating over a radiation bubble or one with three quarters of its population underwater. It doesn't make sense to me.

There was a time when I thought about leaving Hereford. The city imitates a time of peace from our past, but there are others which continue to strive towards the future. I wanted to see the interconnected trains of Europe and the bridges to Africa, but then I met Grey and his wife. They were running from something when I found them. The fear in their eyes convinced me I was fine staying where I was.

"What do you think we should get Charlie for her

birthday?" Ezra reached into his pocket and pulled out a small card.

I paused. "Where is this *we* coming from? She's your sister."

He nodded. "True, but if it sucks and it came from both of us then she has no choice but to like it."

"I'm sorry, what?"

He smiled. "You heard me."

"I think she just wants us to stop destroying her bar."

He shook his head. "Definitely not. That would ruin the intrigue. Everyone knows the Roo is rarely the same from quarter to quarter."

That is when I saw him, long before Ezra did—a man carrying a woman in his arms and walking down a road meant for horses. "Hey! Look out!"

The rider wasn't paying attention. I ran past Ezra and pushed them out of the way as a line of riders hurried past. Seeing the state they were in, I took them to the only place I knew would be able to help.

There were people after them. I defended them without hesitation and didn't bother asking any questions. I realize now that I should have.

The darkness feels as if it's eating away at my sanity. The noises provoke reactions, and while I know I've only been trapped for a few hours, it feels as if it has been days. I'm losing my edge. It's getting harder and harder to keep myself calm.

Without warning, the lights flash back on and I find myself face to face with a malnourished canine. Starving any animal will make them savage. It jumps, and I pull the trigger. Its carcass dissolves into a pool onto the floor.

"Is a snap worth all this trouble?" The speaker lowers, but the voice isn't Grey's. It's the voice from earlier, but way less chipper.

I laugh. "I don't know, you tell me."

I have just a brief window in which to study my surroundings. They only keep the lights on for a couple of minutes at a time. I need to identify something—anything—that will help me get out of here.

The speaker rotates in a full circle. "I'm told there was a time when we considered psychology an artform. The mind is a strange thing. Even those with the will to survive have a breaking point."

I nod. "Everyone has a breaking point."

"I am going to enjoy finding yours." All amusement in the voice is gone. If anything, each word sounds more and more mechanical.

Is Grey messing with my mind? Is there really a second person on the other end of the speaker? I don't know.

Come on, Octavia, think.

I need to find a way out of here soon.

I can feel my sanity slowly slipping away.

19
THE MOTHER AND HER CHILDREN

MY MAMA USED TO TELL ME that first impressions were everything. No matter what happens after that, we subconsciously look back on the initial meeting and recall the qualities which stood out about the person. Those first moments tell us just about everything we need to. This is not an exaggeration.

No matter where we go, Ezra and I always come back to the Roo. It's home, plain and simple. Times like this, when I find myself in the middle of a tight spot, I think of the jukebox and the beer.

"Octavia, please." The speaker crackles in the darkness. "Help us."

The voice is different. Is that a child?

My hands are shaking as the lights come on again.

This room was made for torture. I am sure of it.

"You have to make the favour sound more appealing." I sit, my back against the wall, with my weapon still clenched in my hand. I haven't let it go since this whole thing started. "The way I see it, this is all very one-sided." I take aim at the speaker and pull the trigger. The bullet ricochets as I knew it would.

"Are you finally ready to negotiate?" The voice shifts

again.

I shake my head. "No, I just wanted to mess with you like you're messing with me."

A loud scream echoes from behind me.

There is someone else here.

"The sounds of agony foreshadow your future. Grey insisted we deviate from our regular methods, but our patience is running out." The lights go out again. "This is your last chance to do as we ask. I have no problem giving our usual methods another go."

For a moment, there is silence. Not just the absence of background noise, no. This is true silence. I can't even hear the hum of electricity. Something is different. No panels open, no mixture of real and illusion enters. There is simply nothing. I walk the perimeter, feeling my way based on memory. The panels where the creatures entered were directly across from me. It's hard for me to judge distance when there is nothing for me to see.

I step in something slippery, and freeze. It's thick and viscous. Then, without warning, the lights come on and the speaker lowers. Whatever I've stepped in smells foul. I can't bring myself to look down. It is still eerily quiet.

I take a deep breath, walk towards the speaker, and begin to bash the butt of my pistol against its side.

I need to get out of here.

One of the side panels falls to the ground, exposing several wires. I dig the tip of my pistol behind several and yank them back. The lights flicker, sparks crackle, and one panel opens to a hallway. I move quickly.

A small explosion erupts from the speaker, and the door begins to close.

Go faster, Octavia.

I don't think I've ever sprinted so fast in my life.

I'm not going to make it.

I let go of my pistol and slide, just in time to catch both sides of the door with my hands. I can feel the gears trying to force it closed as I struggle to keep it open. Come on. Every inch it moves takes more effort than it feels like it's worth.

"You're so close." Without warning, Grey kicks through the door's opening and sends me flying back into the room. He pauses at the entrance, pushes a button on the wall, and the door opens without any difficulties.

On his forearms are a pair of vambraces.

I stand and stare only at him. "Get out of my way."

He shakes his head. "I can't do that, Octavia. I have no—"

"Don't give me some bullshit excuse about not having a choice. I'm not in a mood to hear it."

"But it's the truth." He sighs. "What I do, I do for her."

There is a moment where the room feels like it's moving again.

"Do you even know how to use those?"

He nods and touches the wires woven into the leather. "I had to learn, to survive."

I watch as he brings the palm of his left hand down onto his fist and activates the weapon around his wrists. My eyes widen. I've only seen one other Brigand summon weapons like that. A large shotgun appears in his hands. "Grey, what did you do?"

"I don't expect you to understand how fragile business can be. It's either feast or famine. I used to supply weapons to all the settlements from British Columbia to Saskatchewan." He sighs. "When St. Joseph's fell, business died out, and I learned a very important lesson." He pauses. "Never trust Paladins. They're the reason I'm forced to live on Hereford, out of Voltza's jurisdiction."

I step backwards. "Are you going to shoot me?"

He shakes his head. "I don't want to."

I recognize the weapon he's holding.

Valentin.

A surge of rage flows through me as I snap my fingers, pulling the trigger the moment it materializes in my hand. Grey reacts as expected and does the same. Three bullets fly towards him, but two shells of pellets make their way towards me. I dive to the side but feel a sharp pain in my right shoulder.

Grey staggers backwards and lets go of his weapon. An arrogant smirk spreads across his face as he looks down at the wound in his abdomen. "They say it's impossible to see a Brigand draw." He laughs and presses hard against his wound. "But I saw you, Octavia. You're no better than the rest of us."

I watch as he steps backwards and closes the door between us. The speaker sparks, and I am left waiting for something to happen. The blood is fresh, and the air starts to feel heavy. Then the lights go out again; the darkness returns. I'm going to kill him. That is a promise.

20
THE LAWS OF HEREFORD

I'VE NEVER FEARED BEING LOCKED IN A CAGE. Confinement is just a puzzle waiting to be solved. The wires I pulled earlier provoked a very prompt response for someone to come in and intervene. I must focus my efforts there. The constant changing of dark and light is disorienting, to say the least.

I take off my shirt and inspect the wound on my shoulder. It's sore, but not horrible. I'm lucky, plain and simple. I do my best to create a bandage, but I'm no doctor.

"Do you know what this room was originally created for, Octavia?" Grey's muffled voice echoes from the other side of the door.

I don't answer him.

He continues. "It's a replica of an interrogation room built after the global conflict of—"

I shake my head. "What does it matter?"

"It's rude to interrupt people." He laughs. "But I'm sure you know your history. We found this gem and decided to give it a try. You Brigands are tough, and getting what we wanted was very messy." He coughs. "You understand, don't you?"

I don't. "No."

"It's all about family, plain and simple."

Family? I don't have one anymore, but I remember exactly what it was like when I did. Ezra and his family have a dynamic I've never witnessed before, but I enjoy being around them. And then there is Valentin.

Valentin.

I take a deep breath. "You understand that you attacked my family, don't you?" There is only silence from the other side of the door. "I am owed retribution. For all of it."

The lights go out again and this time I close my eyes. The familiar sound of snapping echoes around the room and I feel my vambraces fall from my wrists.

The door opens, and all I can see is the silhouette of a woman. "That took too long, Grey." Grey steps into view behind her. "We should have treated her like the others."

I recognize the voice.

Harriet.

He shakes his head. "A debt is a debt. She saved our lives."

She nods. "Business is business, though."

"I'm sorry, my dear, but in this case you're wrong."

They aren't taking my weapons. I pause, pick up my vambraces, and pull the main circuit boards from the underside of their modulators. My shoulder throbs as I stand and toss the vambraces aside.

Harriet rolls her eyes. "What a waste..." She pauses. "...of time." The lights come back on as she walks into the interrogation room. She looks up and down before her gaze stays on me. "Don't even think about using that." She points to the knife in my boot. "I will slit your throat with it before you have the chance to move."

Everything about her feels wrong. This isn't the woman I've come to know over the years. Grey pushes himself off the wall and comes in after her. He still clutches his wound with both hands. I lean back and sigh. "So, it was all an act then? Wanting to become citizens of Hereford?"

Harriet shakes her head. "Of course not. We came here out of necessity. Voltza's reach is endless. You think we're the first criminals to evade the prison and settle here? The laws of this city keep us safe. We don't wrong anyone here, no one would ever ask questions."

I take a deep breath. "But now you have wronged people."

She nods. "Out of necessity. There are some parts of our past which have caught up with us."

Grey walks towards me and picks up what's left of my vambraces. "We need weapons to address what is coming."

She pauses. "It's nothing personal."

"That's where you're wrong." I stand as Harriet draws a weapon. "You just made it personal."

Without warning, the doors close, and for the first time since waking up in this room, I feel as if I have an advantage. The lights flicker, and Harriet looks to Grey as if he might have an answer for what is happening.

She turns towards me and takes aim. "Enough of this."

But the lights go off as she pulls the trigger.

◆◆◆

History tells us that those who broke laws were deemed criminals of society. The whole system of bringing these criminals to justice was long, tedious, and sometimes unrewarding. It was flawed, and back then it seemed like no one knew how to fix it. When the cities were created, the Maverick claimed Voltza's justice would be different. Rehabilitation was to be its focus. In the end, it's still just a prison. Justice takes far too long.

Ezra has always been a contented man. He derives pleasure from the simple things more than anyone else I've ever known.

"When are you going to give yourself some time to chill?" Ezra paused. "You're going to burn yourself out."

I knew this and yet I didn't want to listen.

Most times when I felt extreme fatigue were one hundred percent my own fault. "Maybe."

He picked up the beer in his hand. "Not maybe. It always happens. This is phase one: denial."

"Really? Bringing out the sarcasm and everything?"

He nodded. "Have you met me? You knew what you were getting into when we first started this partnership."

I shook my head. "Just drink your beer. We've got things that need doing."

He laughed and laughed before involuntarily choking on his beer. "You're your own worst enemy, Octavia."

"I know, but it hasn't killed me yet."

The room is dark and it's quiet. I don't want to move. Not yet, anyway. I carefully slide the hunting knife out of my boot and wait. Both Grey and Harriet are frantic.

"What's going on?" She turns towards the door but stops as it closes in front of her.

We are surrounded by darkness.

Grey steps towards the middle of the room. "Did you get her or not?"

I take care to control my breathing.

"I think so."

Strange scratching noises echo all around us. I recognize this as one of the room's illusions. Everything from the smell to the sounds are meant to chip away at your mind. I slowly move to a crouched position and listen to how Grey and Harriet are moving. This isn't over, and the last thing I want to do is ruin the element of surprise.

"Octavia, are you alright?" Ezra's voice booms overhead.

Both Grey and Harriet scramble back towards the door. I don't say anything as I make my way towards them.

"Octavia, please. Answer me. I don't know what I'm doing—"

The lights come on, and I grab the first person I see.

Grey's eyes meet mine only seconds before I plunge the hunting knife into his throat. Specks of red splatter all over my face as he falls. Harriet reacts by pointing a gun towards me. Her hand is shaking, and her eyes are only on her husband. I grab the barrel and kick her backwards. She falls just outside the door into the hallway.

A muffled explosion erupts above us.

"This won't end with us." She stands and slams her palm against the wall. "We're not alone."

The doors slam shut, and I am left standing in a

mess. "I know."

Ezra's voice still calls out over the speaker. "Octavia?"

"I'm fine, Ezra." But he still continues to call out.

He can't hear me.

I touch my face. It feels wet, and when I look down, I see nothing but red on my fingers.

It might be better this way.

21
THE MEANING OF JUSTICE

Ezra once told me there are some parts of our history that humanity is better off not knowing about. Is this why the infrastructure exists beneath Hereford? So we can hide the things we aren't proud of? Torture is inhumane. I, along with millions of others, know this—and yet human history is proof that we weren't above using it. This room is no exception. I have no doubt that I am still on Hereford, especially considering that I recognize the markings from the wall in the hallway. They are the same as when I descended beneath the Citadel with Valentin and Fynn before.

I must be in the tunnels.

This must be where the Chroniclers put things worth forgetting about.

"Octavia?" Ezra keeps calling out over the speaker over and over again as if my silence on the airwaves will change. I was talking to Grey over some kind of microphone before, but my bet is that it was part of the speaker I tore apart.

I take a deep breath and kneel next to Grey's body. He must have something on him that will help me get out of this room.

"Ezra, did you find Valentin?" Asher's voice is softer, but still echoes over the speaker system.

"He's somewhere in the same wing as Octavia. I just... there's only one active room, and I can't..."

I pull a keycard from Grey's pocket and walk towards the door. "Come on, what good is this if there's no—"

The doors open quickly, and I don't hesitate to jump through them. Ezra is probably pushing every button in front of him. I shove the keycard in my pocket and take a moment to familiarize myself with my surroundings. The hall is bright, lined with several images and placards dating back to the pre-millennium. I don't care about this lost history. All I need to do is find Valentin.

Asher and Ezra's conversation is muffled and confined only to the room I was just in. I raise the gun in my hand and cautiously move forward down the hall. I am on full alert. Everything about this situation has me ready to pull the trigger.

Another explosion echoes.

What is going on up there?

There are three rooms to my left, all with the same placards as the interrogation room I just stepped out of. There on the right-hand side of each one is a key card panel. I pause long enough to check the magazine in my pistol. It's old, but in immaculate condition.

About a dozen rounds left.

I open the first door and am hit with a distinctly foul odour. The lights turn on as I step inside. In the middle of the room is a body, torn apart and decomposing. I look away, back out, and close the door behind me.

A loud bang echoes from room number two.

I open the door and see a Brigand in tattered gear. He turns, slowly, and then stops. We've never met, but I can tell there's something wrong.

"Old men are broken too easily. That's what they said. That's what they said... when... when..." His demeanour changes. "When they came from the sky."

I keep my weapon raised. "Who are—"

He raises a hand and I see the scratch marks all over his arms where his vambraces should be. "The sky doesn't know what it is like to be grounded. Wouldn't you agree? Wouldn't you?"

I take a deep breath. "What is your name?"

He pauses. "That is none of your concern."

I stagger back as he growls and begins an aggressive sprint towards me. Instinct takes over. I pull the trigger twice, and he plummets to a halt just short of the door. A loud bang echoes from door number three, and despite my hesitation, I open it, ready to find absolutely anything on the other side. What I see forces me to lower my weapon.

There at the edge of the room is Valentin, sitting with his legs close to his chest. He doesn't look up as I walk towards him. The floor is flooded with about an inch of water. "Valentin."

He doesn't answer.

Fear is powerful. Everyone is afraid of something, and whatever that *something* is should not be trifled with. I walk into this room and feel just how afraid Valentin must have been. His arms are bare, and the water around him has a slight red hue to it. He only looks up as I kneel directly in front of him.

"Octavia?"

I nod and take a seat at his side. The water is cool to the touch. "Don't worry, I'm right here. We'll move when you're ready to."

I've spent a good part of my adult life letting old men tell me what to do. It was all part of the job: an expectation for those who strived to be Brigands on Hereford. There weren't many of us then, and there aren't many of us now. I can't help but think that we are mostly extinct, and for what? So a convicted arms dealer could acquire new technology? Grey told me it was just business, but I call bullshit on that.

Valentin walks with a slight limp. I saw it the moment he finally stood and followed me out into the hall. We are Brigands, and while we have both had our fair share of scrapes, this one is different. This one is personal. Even we need time to recover. I hope he's alright.

Another explosion erupts. "What is going on up there?" Valentin walks into my old torture room, approaches Grey's corpse and retrieves his vambraces.

I pause. "It sounds like anarchy."

He shakes his head. "It sounds like a warzone."

Those echoing explosions remind me of the battle on Voltza.

Steady footsteps approach from the hall. Both Valentin and I react accordingly.

We take aim towards the door as Asher walks into view with a small orange firearm in his hands.

He drops it as soon as he sees us. "Don't shoot!"

I lower my weapon. "Where's Ezra?"

Asher pauses. "One floor up. He's still trying to figure out what all the switches and buttons do." He then looks at Valentin. "Are you alright?"

Valentin nods. "I'll be fine."

Asher picks up his weapon and motions to the hall. "Then we have to get Ezra and make our way back up to the surface. It's getting rowdy out there."

The ground shakes for a brief moment as another explosion erupts. Rowdy sounds like an understatement.

22
THE REEL OF TIME

I DON'T CARE WHAT ANYONE SAYS,, business is not separate from personal affairs. It never has been and never will be. The path we take in life is of our own choosing. On Hereford, all roads lead to the Citadel, including this one. My mama always said that having one home is a myth, and that anyone can have more than one if they desired. Any place can be a home. It's as simple as that.

"Are you alright?" Ezra walks slower than usual. I can feel him staring.

I nod. "Yes, of course. Why wouldn't I be?"

He pauses. "It's just…"

"Ezra."

He stops in his tracks.

"You're safe. That's all that matters."

"That's not true." He clears his throat. "You matter. I don't care what Mason says, both you and Valentin are just as important as Asher and I are. We're a team. Always."

I smile. "No need to get sappy on me."

Asher and Ezra lead us through the halls as if they've been here before. Some of the displays we pass are more than a little disturbing.

"One of the things we struggle with is just how much of our history we should make common knowledge." Asher motions to one of the rooms on the left. "I'm not perfect, but some events make me look like a saint. How messed up is that?"

Valentin stops and looks at a placard. "All history should be common knowledge." He pauses. "Shouldn't it?"

Ezra shakes his head. "It's not that simple."

"The past is what influences our future." I turn. "It should all be accessible."

It becomes clear to me, in this moment, that there are procedures and philosophies at play which I wasn't aware existed. I've always tried not to trouble myself with these things, and yet, here they are.

Should I have paid more attention?

Maybe.

It's hard to say. There's a side to the Chroniclers which I still have no desire to immerse myself in, but that choice is being taken from me. Life is getting a little too complicated. I miss the days when all I had to do was worry about protecting one person. Now it feels like my job is about more than that.

As we walk, the silence is uneasy.

The four of us have never been so quiet, and Ezra and I have never had this much tension between us.

◆

"You're safe. That's all that matters. Don't ever go against my orders again!" Mason's words are directed at Asher and Ezra—not at Valentin, and certainly not at me. "You two need to understand—"

"Where's Fynn?" I look around the Roo and see a room full of Chroniclers. There are no patrons, and Charlie looks less than impressed.

"Go on, tell her." She shakes her head. "Where's the man from Voltza?"

Mason turns away. "He is not our problem."

I step towards him. "Excuse me?"

He pauses. "These are matters you shouldn't be concerning yourself with."

"I'm hearing that a lot lately."

It doesn't look like anyone wants to say anything.

Except for Charlie.

She looks furious. "I think I've had enough of this. Everyone, out!"

All the Chroniclers turn and look at her as if she had just said something sacrilegious.

Mason gasps. "What did you just—"

"Did I fucking stutter? Out. Now." She pauses. "I need to have a word with my brothers." Mason glares at her. "In private."

Another explosion rings out in the distance.

It sounds close.

Valentin and I look at each other.

"Relax." She turns to the two of us. "Those aren't what you think they are."

"What do you mean?" I can't help but grip the pistol on my hip.

She sighs. "Hereford has been drifting without anyone noticing. We're so high that both Voltza and St. Joseph's are below us."

Explosions on the cities below us?

Ezra nods. "We don't know what's going on, but it isn't our priority."

Valentin shrugs. "And what is?"

Asher pulls out a chair. "This city. We don't have the resources to worry about anyone other than ourselves."

Many of the Chroniclers have filed out, but Mason lingers at the door. Charlie hops over the bar and marches towards him. "I'm only going to say this one more time. Out!" He hurries out the door.

When it is just the five of us, no one speaks right away. There has been too much left unspoken. I'm not sure if anyone knows where to start.

Ezra clears his throat. "There was a vote which happened while the two of you were missing." He pauses. "About the future of Hereford now that it's clear we aren't in a position of power anymore. We've lost almost all our Brigands. It currently isn't safe to continue our mission."

Asher nods. "That, and the fact we let ourselves be humiliated by criminals. Grey and Harriet are just the start, and their reasoning was petty at best. They made us look like fools—an entire tier of the city."

Ezra leans against the bar. "History shows us that these are the signs of necessary change. Not all of us are willing to go in that direction, though."

Of course not.

Charlie rolls her eyes. "Honestly, I don't care

what goes down politically, but this crime has to stop, and the first step is getting that enhanced man to help us figure out where we stand with the rest of the cities."

Fynn.

"Where is he?" I look to Valentin.

Asher shrugs. "And now you understand the problem. We don't know."

I feel as though we are all at a dead end. I'm trying to pinpoint where everything started changing. Has it always been this way? Maybe I should have cared more about what we were doing. Maybe I should have been more suspicious about those around me. Grey was a friend—at least, that's how I thought of him. It just goes to show how people will never be above surprising you.

I take a deep breath and make my way to the door.

Valentin follows.

Asher calls out, "Where are you two going?"

I pause. "To Grey's gun shop."

23
THE BONDS OF MARRIAGE

HUMANS ARE STRANGE CREATURES. We have a nature which is as equally confusing as it is necessary for our survival. Still, there's one constant which outweighs all others.

Family.

Blood or otherwise, it doesn't matter.

I remember the first time I was in Grey's gun shop. It was also the first time I had ever properly spoken to Harriet. Based on that first impression, I would have told everyone that she was a kind and caring woman.

"I... I just wanted to say thank you. My husband and I... Well, we aren't used to there being kind strangers." Her hair was loose, but still looked perfect.

I nodded and went back to looking around the shop. "No worries. I had no idea you two were gunsmiths. All these replicas..."

"Grey is really talented, and a bit of a fanatic when it comes to gunpowder weapons. I prefer magnetic propulsion. Everyone has their preference." She paused. "But I do believe mine is the best."

I shrugged and picked up an M1911. "How much for this one?"

She smiled. "For you? It's on the house."

There's one stop we have to make before we head to Grey's. Valentin walks slowly behind me as we make our way through the front door of a house I haven't set foot in for several months. Ezra and I have been travelling like nomads for so long that I found more convenience sleeping in Charlie's guest room above the Roo. This place feels both familiar and foreign.

"Make yourself comfortable. I won't be long."

Valentin nods and pulls out a chair in the kitchen. This house is too big for me. Always has been and always will be.

"You ever heard of the wild west? Asher was telling me about it before all this shit blew up in our faces." Valentin sighs.

I pull a small metal box from under my bed. "I have. It's the basis for Hereford's laws."

"What if it's wrong, and that's why every other city is unified under a different set of rules?"

I take a deep breath, open the box, and pull out a holstered pistol and gun belt. "It doesn't matter. If there's one thing the last few days have shown us, it's that our current way of life isn't sustainable anymore."

"Then we should leave."

I turn and see him leaning up against the door frame. "There's no shame in wanting to survive."

He nods. "No, there isn't."

I take off my shirt and carefully adjust the bandage on my shoulder. My scars are visible. I know he can see them. When I look back, I see that he's turned to face the wall. "It's alright, you know. You don't have to look away."

There is a moment of stillness which drifts between us. The look on his face tells me he has no idea how to react. I smile and continue on as if nothing has happened. I hear his footsteps cross the room as I grab a new shirt from my dresser and carefully put it on. My shoulder still hurts, but it's more than manageable.

"Octavia." Valentin stands at the window with his arms crossed. "There are some things we've never talked about."

I nod. "There always are."

"Can we talk about them?"

"Of course." I pick up the metal box and walk towards the door. "After we've dealt with Harriet."

Intuition is not something you can train yourself to have. On the contrary, everyone is born with it. My mama always said that it's a person's greatest weapon. No guns or bullets can ever compare. We walk, together, through doorways and past faded paintings until there's nothing left between us but those unspoken things we really should talk about. I tighten the holster, and start filling the mags.

The hunt starts now.

♦

When I kick open the front door to Grey's gun shop, I have my pistol in one hand and a hunting knife in the other. Valentin summons his weapon and follows behind me. This place feels eerie and off. Something is different, and I can't help but try to analyse what it is. It is quiet, without even the slight hum of electricity from the overhead lights.

Valentin goes to the far wall and starts fiddling with the breaker, but it's no use. He throws down a handful of wires and turns back. The power is off, and someone went through a lot of trouble to make sure it stayed that way.

Explosions still echo below us.

What the hell is going on down there?

"Octavia." Valentin motions towards the closed door behind the secondary counter. A faint light is visible through the crack between the wood and the floor.

I nod and move towards it.

One kick, and the door crashes open.

"What the—"

We walk in and all the lights flicker on. In the middle of the room is a table with a large sheet covering a lump no longer than a meter. All the cabinets and tools make the room look more like a surgical unit than anything else. The walls and floors are spotless. Someone was quick to clean this place.

"Don't go any further," a voice whispers from behind us. I turn and see Harriet, eyes bloodshot, holding a pistol to Valentin's head. Her breathing is shallow and she looks like she has been crying. "Put your weapons on the ground."

"What do you attempt to gain with all of this?" I slowly do as she says. "You must need something, or else you would have cut and run."

"What I need... is in the past now." She pauses. "It was supposed to be just business, but you made it personal."

I shake my head. "I made it personal? Tell me, what about this entire thing wasn't personal to begin with? You and Grey—"

She moves the pistol from Valentin's head to his arm and pulls the trigger. "Don't say his name."

My eyes widen as he cries out. "Valentin..."

The pistol in her hand starts to shake. "You have no right. None, you hear me?"

Two more gunshots ring out.

It happens that fast.

I scream because my brain registers only one thing as both Valentin and Harriet fall to the ground. My heart races as I hurry towards them.

"What a mess." Mason sighs and starts walking towards me with a gun in his hand. "This whole thing is unacceptable."

There is no mistaking the rage in his eyes.

24
THE MINISTER'S MUSIC BOX

Hereford is the only city without a security force. Our laws are simple and mean that every citizen oversees their own justice. As I look at the man across from me, all I can think about are numbers and statistics. How quick can I get my gun off the floor? What is the probability of him being able to shoot me when I dive for it? Is Valentin...

I'm not one to cry unless someone else starts crying first. Tears can be powerful, but only in the presence of the right audience. Everything about this scene feels wrong, and the man staring at me with a gun in his hand is furious. I don't know how to read the situation. For the first time in a long while, I don't know if there is a right or wrong decision to make here.

"Is this a game to you?" Mason looks to me, kicks Harriet's corpse aside, and then nudges Valentin with his boot. "Or you? This isn't how we handle things. Not when the fate of the city hangs in the balance."

Valentin struggles to sit up. "Mason?"

He nods. "Get up. This whole thing is a bloody

mess."

A surge of questions flood through my mind.

"You said the city hangs in the balance. The balance of what exactly?" I watch as Mason moves closer. "We create our own justice in this city."

He shrugs. "Only to a certain point."

"What are you talking about?"

He pauses. "I don't expect you to understand the politics."

I look down at my pistol. "There are no politics involved here. This is simply a matter of—"

"Think about what you're about to say, Octavia. I am not in the mood to squabble."

There is a look in Mason's eyes which I've never seen before. Desperation—I recognize it instantly. I can't quote famous figures of history or recite the oaths of our ancestors, but I know stories, and not one of them involving a desperate person ever ended well. Desperate people are capable of anything. Mason is no different. The room goes silent as Valentin stands. This room feels more and more uneasy with every passing moment.

Mason saunters past me with his pistol loose in his hand. I consider disarming him, but don't because it's obvious his attention has shifted to whatever is under the sheet on the table. "My grandfather helped build this city." He pauses. "Took the concept from blueprint to reality." He takes a deep breath. "He said humans have always set their own limits. Why should the cities be any different?"

Valentin puts pressure on the wound in his arm and steps beside me. "Mason, it's over. We can go back to—"

He sets down his pistol and gently lifts the edge of the sheet. A few moments pass as he starts to weep. "No, we can't."

I pick up my weapons from the floor and walk towards Mason. The closer I get, the clearer the situation comes. I know what's on the table before I can see it for myself. On the floor in a pan next to one end is a pile of wires, metal plating, and screws. I take the edge of the sheet from Mason and pull it back in one swift motion. There, face up, is Fynn, all his synthetic parts harvested and removed. He looks like a dissected piece of meat.

I place two fingers against his neck.

He is cold.

"This changes everything."

I am no stranger to death. Valentin and I are Brigands. We've seen and caused much death in our lives. My mama once told me that it's good for everyone to feel their mortality every now and then. It keeps us honest.

I walk closer to the Maverick's son and see just how much technology was in his body--all of which is probably still in this room. The pan is overflowing, and the silhouettes of separated limbs rest under a second sheet on one of the counters opposite the door. I'm lost in thought until Mason's voice breaks the silence.

"This is your fault." He pulls the sheet back into place and looks me squarely in the eye. "You shouldn't have brought him here."

A good portion of the events from the last couple of days runs through my mind. "Are we going to start this again?"

He pauses. "We're in an impossible position now. You should have known."

I shake my head. "Should have known what? That two people would attack the Citadel to further their business? That Hereford has a city's worth of levels beneath the surface where it hides dark parts of our history? Or are you referring to the fact that we are at a point of change?"

He pauses. "The Maverick will come for his son."

I nod. "Of course he will—"

"And it will be the end for all of us."

He turns away and looks towards what's left of Fynn's body. There it is again, desperation. I watch as he pulls a lighter out of his pocket and I know exactly what he's about to do.

"Mason, you can't cover this up."

He brings up his gun. "Watch me."

There was a time when I believed in fairy tales and happy endings. The finales of those stories were always emotional and left the audience feeling good about the journey taken by the characters. They were also horribly unrealistic. As I watch Mason, I feel a sense of reckoning. My story is about to end. I've seen enough death to know mine is only seconds away.

He pulls the trigger.

I do the same.

Valentin screams at me, but I can't hear his words. I hit the ground and find myself looking up at the ceiling. There is a hand holding mine, and soon I'm staring not at ceiling tiles, but at Valentin.

His eyes are watering.
Does he have something in them?
Then he kisses me, and I know.
Is this what love feels like?
I've never been in love before.

25
THE MESSENGER'S CUBE

THE WORD FOREVER IS HIGHLY MISLEADING. It is simply something which cannot exist. There isn't anything else to it. Nothing is infinite, even though we might want it to be. It is inevitable that everyone's time will run out eventually.

I don't know how, and I don't know why, but between a blink and a breath I find myself standing in a field of green grass overlooking the western end of Hereford. There aren't many buildings here. Never have been. There are only horses, and farmers inspecting the vegetation pods. None of them acknowledge my presence.

Can they see me?

"Brigand number 9, can you hear me?" A woman's voice speaks, but as I look around I can't see from where.

I take a deep breath. "I..."

"Please speak louder. The binary sensors aren't the best form of communication."

I turn and see a woman standing tall behind me. Her eyes scream a sadness which could only come from losing someone close. She wears a suit similar to Captain Dawes', and her left hand is covered by a black glove. I have no doubt it is metal.

"Where am I?" I pause. "This looks like Hereford, but it doesn't feel like it."

She nods. "It is Hereford. Every blade of grass, every horse, every building, it's all Hereford."

I reach out with my hand. "Then why can't I feel the air?"

"Because you're a projection travelling without a body." She motions downwards to a small cube emanating light at my feet.

I step away from it, but stop as my arm flickers. "What is—"

She walks forward and picks up the cube. The light continues to create my image. "Many years ago, scientists on St. Joseph's discovered a link between neurocircuitry and human nerves. The brain sends signals like pushing buttons on a computer. That one discovery allowed us to link the mind to circuits in ways we hadn't been able to previously. With the right technology, we can communicate and walk across the world as long as you stay within proximity of the emitter."

I sigh. "So where am I actually?"

"Physically? In a bed on Voltza. Mentally? With me on Hereford."

"Why?"

She starts walking, and I have no choice but to follow. "Because I have questions to ask which only you can answer, and you are not in the best state to help me from the prison."

The roads are empty, and in the distance, I can see the skeleton of the Citadel reaching up towards the sky. It looks fuller than before, as if repairs have been underway for some time. This woman walks with a purpose. Every move she makes looks deliberate. Over her right hand looks to be a weapon similar to my vambraces.

"Fynn Ridley was my brother, and I need help understanding what happened to him. Will you—" She stops abruptly and puts her left hand to her head. "No, don't pull her out. I'm not finished yet."

But it all goes black, and I could swear I hear a curse or two as Hereford blurs out of focus.

"You two are proving to be more trouble than I originally anticipated. You know that, don't you?" The Maverick's voice fills the room. "I'm not a patient man. Especially when it comes to family matters."

A hand squeezes mine, long before I open my eyes. My chest feels heavy and the air is dense. It takes my eyes several moments to adjust to the light shining over my head.

Valentin is there. He sits beside me on a chair which is too small for him. "I don't know what else you want from us. I told you everything I remember."

He's afraid.

The Maverick nods and steps towards us. "Yes, but only she can tell me what she remembers. Testimonies are crucial to judgment. This is the way of the Twelve. No one is guilty without evidence. The more witnesses who speak, the more complete the story."

"While you're here with us, Mason is…" Valentin stops talking as I struggle to sit up. "Octavia? Be careful."

A moment of panic floods through me.

I can't feel my legs.

Tears well up in my eyes. "I don't…"

"My daughter spoke to you, didn't she?" The Maverick reaches into his pocket and pulls out a small cube.

I nod. "Yes, but—"

He sighs. "Her methods are much different than mine. She thinks she can handle this on her own, just like everything else in her life. I am going to ask you one question and one question only. How you answer it will determine the actions I take on not just Hereford, but on all citizens within the twelve. Do you understand?"

I don't say anything.

"Now, wait just a minute." Valentin lets go of my hand.

The Maverick shakes his head. "I've made many mistakes in my life, but this might be the largest of them." He pauses for a moment, and I could swear that beneath all the metal is a man who wants to cry but can't. "Tell me what happened to my son. I need to hear it from you."

My mama always told me to be wary of a man who grieves. His actions will not be his own, and his words will be twisted by emotions he never knew he had.

Here, standing in front of me, is the almighty Maverick—Elias Ridley. His tears are invisible, and no matter what citizens say, I can see his heart through all the wires and all the metal.

What do you say to a parent who just lost their child?

I don't know. I really... don't know.

~TJL~

VIOLENT SKIES **URBAN HEROES** **GUNMETAL GREYS**

WHAT'S NEXT?

INTRODUCING

If you enjoyed GUNMETAL GREYS,
be on the lookout for

THE NATURE OF GODS

T.J. LOCKWOOD

1
THE COUNCIL OF HEROES

THIS PATH HAS SEEN MANY BATTLES. Centuries of dirt compacted by the heels of military boots is enough to make every inch of the ground erode a little more with each step. It doesn't matter who you are or where you come from, we're all stepping on fragile soil. I hear the thunder bellowing over the mountains. The air is saltier than it used to be. It's been a long time since I've walked this way, but when it comes to traveling between countries, this is the route I always take. It's longer than going by cart or train. The peace is what I enjoy the most. No one comes through here unless they enjoy the silence and the occasional storm.

When I was several centuries younger, the fields were green with a farmer's grass and a merchant's money. I could smell the crops at the height of their season and the horses waiting in their stables, but not anymore. This world is very much black and white now. Perhaps part of that is my fault. This place was created as an adventure: an attempt to survive. I suppose all things must come to an end eventually, but for people like me, time is far too generous. My steps are empty, shifting the ground and leaving only mere imprints in its dust. Soon the wind will come and there will be nothing again. That's how it always is, and perhaps that's how it always should be.

"Ma'am, could you spare a coin? I haven't eaten in days." A beggar kneels at a fork in the road. I've seen him before, in the country next to this one. Sometimes he preaches ideals I'm almost certain he doesn't fully comprehend. He's a small, frail, man with coin in his pockets. A beggar? Hardly. He claims to need food, but there is no mistaking the tomato juice dried on the corners of his mouth. Perhaps he means for it to look like blood, but I know the difference. One doesn't walk this way without seeing one's fair share of red.

"And if I give you a coin, you will only get hungrier." I don't make eye contact; instead, I turn towards the path leading west.

He pushes himself off the ground and takes several steps in my direction. His balance is horrid at best. "What does that mean?"

I turn and lower my hood. "It means that you would just want more."

He stares, like most do, at the vertical scar on the left side of my face. There's terror in his eyes. His previous steps forward soon become hesitant stumbling backwards. "By the gods... Forgive me—I didn't know."

There are no gods. I pull the hood back over my head. "I suggest you stick to honest work. Beggars don't encounter decent people on this road."

There's no denying his fear. "I... yes. Of course."

I don't look back at him. Gravel shifts frantically and I know he has taken off running down the road heading east. There is a faint whistle in the wind. I have heard it many times before. That man knows only greed. People like him show just how corrupt humans have become.

Perhaps this is our fault.

I continue on for another hour before I feel the silence again. The stars are brighter than they have been all season. With each passing second, I sense a rise in energy. I must be getting close. I know that my destination will be within reach further down this trail. Soon the fog will surround me and I will have to continue on instinct and memory, but I'm not complaining. After all, this is the road I chose to follow.

The tunnel is closer than I remember—either that or my stride has gotten longer; it wouldn't surprise me if that were the case. I'm about a hundred meters away when the large metal door opens. A man comes out slowly. His silver-trimmed black coat matches my own. "You're late."

I continue on. "By whose time?"

He turns back towards the tunnel. "Quit with the sarcasm, Livia. You know what I mean. The others are already inside."

I nod. "Then relax a little. We're all here now."

"I'll relax when I can get back to Osteinberg." His name is Gerard. He and I have known each other for centuries, long before this place existed.

He is a man of structure and punctuality.

"Don't you start about having places to be." I pause and tuck a stray strand of blond hair behind his ear.

"We're already late."

"Then a few more seconds won't matter." I lower my hood. "Our duties aren't going anywhere."

We walk together in perfect stride. Beyond the dark halls is the main interior. From there, we head left into a small conference room. I step inside and am instantly greeted with the attention of my peers. The conversations stop until both Gerard and I take our seats. Each of us is studying the others. I haven't seen many of these faces in a few decades, but that isn't what concerns me; the chair across from mine is empty.

I clear my throat and turm to Gerard. "I thought everyone was here. Where is Henrik?"

To my left, Alessia interjects. The jewels on her fingers could easily pass as weapons. "Tinkering with his robots. Where else would he be?" Bitter as always, but I guess I shouldn't expect anything less when we're talking about her ex-husband.

I lean back in my seat. "If he can have other things occupy his time, then why can't the rest of us do the same? His absence is insulting."

"Let him be. The man is incapable anyway." Demetrius, the man across from Alessia, sits with his arms folded. His eyes are as golden as the skies used to be.

I turn away. "You know I hate double standards."

Gerard gestures for silence. "I think that's

enough. We have more important things to discuss." He turns to his right. "Marcus, what is our progress with the Eastern front?"

Marcus shrugs. "Nothing has changed. It's holding, as usual."

These discussions never bear much fruit. Every century we gather and sit. As far as I'm concerned, it's nothing more than obligatory small talk. Each of my fellow Generals cares only about their separate countries. I don't blame them. The lust for new territories died a long time ago. I sit, head resting on my fist, and listen to the pointless chatter. To me the sign of a great leader is how their followers act in their absence. I'm not sure if the others agree with my philosophy.

"It's about time someone checked on Ivan, don't you think?" Those words come from the shorter man to my left: Erik. He speaks to no one in particular. Still, his question attracts our full attention.

Alessia taps her fingers impatiently on the table. "And who should go this time? Arthur? I believe it's your turn isn't it?"

Arthur takes a sip of his wine and sets the glass back on its coaster. "Why would I go to such a dreadful place?"

"Because it's your turn." Juliana twirls her knife between her fingers. "Don't think you're getting out of it this time."

Arthur sighs. "I just don't enjoy being in that country. It's too dark for my liking."

I sigh. "It's fine. I'll go."

Marcus leans forward. "Are you sure, Livia? Didn't you just come from his country?"

I nod. "No, I came from the North this time. I'm not opposed to seeing him. Besides, I think any message this council has will be better received if it comes from me."

A moment of silence surrounds all of us. Everyone here knows exactly what I'm talking about; the Great Divide. This table once held thirteen seats, but that was so long ago. I haven't forgotten what has been written into history, nor am I one to merely push it aside. Ivan and I have a mutual understanding when it comes to discussing the past, and that is why I have no problem visiting our former comrade.

"Then it's settled. We will reconvene in a century's time." Gerard is the first to stand.

One by one the Generals file out of the room until only Juliana and I are still in our seats. "Is something bothering you?"

She shakes her head. "No, I'm just thinking."

"About what?"

She slides her knife back into its sheath. "Just the things I have to do when I get back. Storm season is coming."

I stand. "I guess you're right."

She smiles and turns to the exit. "So, will you be back in your country soon, or am I still looking after it?"

"If it has become a problem—"

"It's no problem; I just want to know so the people don't think that their divine leader has abandoned them."

My expression changes. "The people can take care of themselves. That is what I have helped them accomplish. If we keep babying them, they'll be casualties in the wake of evolution. I still think this planet should be left to them to do as they please."

She sighs. "You have too much faith in humans. It shows in your country. Your republic is a little too opinionated for my taste."

I step past her. "We will see. There will come a time when they won't need us."

She takes off her gloves and claps her hands together. "Whatever you say, Livia. Let me know when you're back."

"I will."

I watch as her aura changes to a dark green. The rise in energy is familiar to me. After all, it is this control over the world that makes us Generals. She runs, leaving only a small cloud of dust where she once was. I smile and continue towards the door. Juliana's speed is legendary, but I prefer to take my time with such things as travel.

"Always the show-off, isn't she?" Demetrius is waiting for something. He leans against the wall with a look of boredom on his face.

I shrug. "She is gifted with speed; why not use it?"

"We all have abilities, but that doesn't mean we should flaunt them."

"You're one to talk, Demetrius."

He turns. "And so are you, Livia."

I brush past him. "Is there something you wanted?"

"Actually, there is." We walk together. "I was wondering if I could borrow Glaucus."

I don't look at him. "Why?"

He steps in front of me, blocking my path. "For

educational purposes. I promise."

"And to whom would you be teaching the art of war to?"

He smiles. "You should trust me more."

I laugh and step around him. "I tried that one already, or have you forgotten?"

"Is that a no?"

I nod. "That is a no."

He sighs. "What a shame. Well, I suppose there's no changing your mind."

"Correct."

He turns towards the large metal door leading out of the tunnel. The sun is out now. It shines down with such vigor. "That's too bad, Livia. It would have been great for the two of us to work together again."

I watch as he steps out into the open air. The sun hits his body and creates an aura similar to Juliana's. I watch as the light grows brighter than any human can stare into. He smiles and the flash dissipates until there is nothing. "And you say Juliana is a show-off."

My attention turns back to the path I had walked on my way here. It seems that, as I was the last to arrive, I am also the last to leave. I pull my hood back up and take the first steps on the worn-out road. I wish it would rain. Things are always better when it rains.

It's colder than usual. The wind was carrying a warm current not two hours ago, but this forest isn't the most hospitable of places. I should have been out of it by now; I must have missed the border gates. I reach under my jacket and pull a small headset from the inside pocket. Once it's settled on my head, I adjust the half visor and turn on the mic. "Glaucus."

An image of an owl appears over my left eye. "Yes, Master?"

I continue forward. "Could you scan the area for me please?"

"Of course." The owl disappears.

I hear a shuffling of gravel to my left. My instincts take over. I jump off the trail and press my back against a tree. I reach to the holster on the back of my belt and pull my pistol from its sheath. There are multiple voices melding into each other; sounds like there are four humans. In any other country, I would have just walked by without any concerns.

The owl reappears. "Master."

I nod. "Talk to me."

"Four humanoids and two canines are exactly west-northwest of your position. Infrared shows standard gunpowder weapons."

I click off the safety. "When did I cross the border?"

"You entered former General Ivan's country exactly three hundred meters ago."

I peek around the corner. "Calculate the probability of escape without confrontation."

"Based on breathing patterns and gestures, twenty-two percent."

That's higher than I thought it would be. "Thank you, Glaucus."

Normally this wouldn't be a problem, but Ivan's country has been in total anarchy since his imprisonment. People, when given complete freedom, are capable of pretty much anything. Two of those men are in tattered military uniform, while the others look to be mere wanderers. I hold my weapon behind my back, push off the tree, and walk towards them. The dogs bark as I get closer.

One of the wanderers rushes forward with both hands out in front of him. "You can't go any further. It's a war zone."

Both men in uniform widen their eyes and take a step back. I smile at their recognition. "Don't worry about me. I know how to take care of myself."

The other civilian merely studies the expression on the soldier's faces. "Did I miss something?"

I continue walking past them all as if nothing had happened. Explosions, I can hear them mounting in the distance. I bring up my left hand and slowly summon the power which flows through my veins; the power of a race nearing extinction. Behind me the dogs whimper and the men are forced to the ground.

"What the hell is this?" The voice is muffled by the sudden change in atmosphere.

One of the soldiers looks to me. "That's General Livia. The earth bends at her will."

Gravity: it is the natural phenomenon that controls how we move. I feel the weight of the air compressing and expanding. It's becoming heavier than steel. The men groan as I carry on. Their bodies are feeling the massive shift of an entire planet in the area of a small field. I am weightless; I have trained myself to tolerate all forms of pressure. My steps are slow and the gunshots are loud. I look back at the men one last time before focusing on what is in front of me.

A battlefield beckons.

It feels just like home.

WANT TO READ MORE?

VISIT *MECHAPANDAPUBLISHING.COM* FOR ACCESS TO THE FULL CATALOGUE

AND

STAY UP TO DATE WITH NEW RELEASES BY SUBSCRIBING TO OUR NEWSLETTER AT

MECHAPANDAPUBLISHING.COM/SUBSCRIBE/

ABOUT THE AUTHOR

T.J. LOCKWOOD is a speculative and science fiction author born somewhere along the west coast of Canada during a relatively mild summer in comparison to the ones which followed. An avid practitioner of the Martial Arts, she is always up for a friendly match or two when time permits. Her writing has, and always will, dive head first through the many portals of Science Fiction. She lives in Vancouver and enjoys the frequently rainy days common in the lower mainland.

Follow her on Twitter (**@TJLwriting**) or listen to her ramble with the crew of Pondo's Playground (**MechaPandaPublishing.com/pondos-playground**).

THANK YOU FOR READING.

Made in the USA
San Bernardino, CA
11 November 2018